Playing with FIRE

AJ RANNEY

Rudy House Publishing

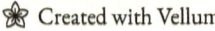

To Cassie: I appreciate all your help and feedback! Logan is officially yours! Enjoy!

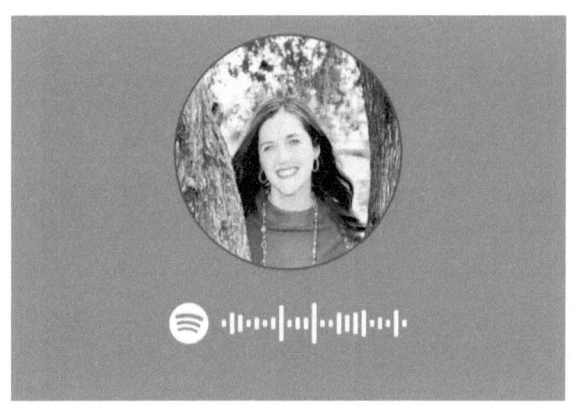

Listen on Spotify!

Play with Fire - Sam Tinnesz, Yacht Money
Kiss Me, Love Me - ORGAVSM
She Loves the Rain - Teddy Swims
The Hotness - Mila Hayes
Hotter Than Hell - Dua Lipa
She Sets The City On Fire - Gavin DeGraw
White Flag - Bishop Briggs
Am I Okay? - Megan Moroney
Worst Way - Riley Green
Fire Meets Gasoline - Sia
The Way I Do - Bishop Briggs
What If I Never Get Over You - Lady A
Make Me Feel - Elvis Drew
Fire Up the Night - New Medicine
You Should Probably Leave - Chris Stapleton

Chapter One

LOGAN

ANOTHER LAUGH ERUPTED from the group of women at the corner table. I picked up my beer and took a long swig, the taste barely registering. My focus was definitely elsewhere. Mostly on the one woman among them I was trying my best to ignore. One who'd wedged herself under my skin in the most frustrating way. Like a stubborn splinter you struggled to get out.

I placed the bottle back down on the table with a thud, and Jay raised a brow at me from across the table. Hopefully, he couldn't see through the mask of indifference I was trying like hell to keep on my face. It was hard enough to hide things from these guys I spent so much time with, but after working with Jay for almost seven years now, he knew me better than most.

"You okay, man?"

I glanced around the table at the rest of the crew, taking in their questioning looks. Shit. Apparently, I was doing a crap job of hiding my frustration tonight.

If it wasn't the new guy's first week with the Half Moon Lake Fire Department, I wouldn't even be making such a strong effort to stay at the bar. Would have found some excuse to get the hell out of here already. But it was only Seth's second day, and it was a hard one.

Another fucking arson case. Third one in the last month and the sixth incident since they started in January. Thankfully, it was always unoccupied buildings, so no civilian injuries. They really needed to solve this shit and figure out who was starting the damn fires before someone ended up seriously hurt. Or worse.

"Yeah. Just a long day." We were all feeling that, and since I couldn't add the real reason I was annoyed, I fell back on the convenient excuse of what we were all thinking. "Ready for them to catch this fucker."

They all nodded and followed it up with another drink of their beers. Seth glanced around the bar. He hadn't said much since we got there. He came across as the quiet type, but I had to wonder if he was regretting taking the job. I hoped not. Because we really needed an extra full-time firefighter.

Nestled in the mountains of North Carolina, Half Moon Lake was an "everyone knew everyone" kind of small town. Our company relied heavily on volunteer firefighters, plus we were routinely short on EMTs. When Adam—who was not only a firefighter, but EMT trained as well—picked up those shifts, it left us a little thin on coverage. And with the chief close to retirement, he was grooming Owen to take his position in a few years, shifting some of his responsibilities and availability as well. Getting Seth up to speed was a bit of a priority, professionally and socially.

Adam stared intently over my shoulder as he took another swig from his bottle. I could tell he was focusing on the same group of women I'd been trying to ignore.

Following his gaze to a brunette I didn't recognize, I tipped my head in that direction. "Why aren't you going over there? You're usually all about that."

He blinked before meeting my gaze and shook his head. "Not like that. She's a student in the EMT class I'm teaching."

Hmm. Interesting. I wasn't buying that he wasn't into her, but I understood the teacher-student issue. In a few weeks, he'd have a new group of students and she would no longer be in his class. Wonder what he'd do then.

I stiffened on my stool as Jay's sister Izzy stepped up to our table, placing three shot glasses down and grabbing two more from her friend behind her. Had they abandoned their table in the corner and decided to come join ours? I couldn't handle anymore torture tonight, and having her so close would definitely be torture.

"You all deserve shots after today." Her long, dirty blonde hair brushed my arm as she turned her head away from me, sending a cascade of curls over her shoulder.

I bit back a groan. Jesus. At this point, maybe I could bail.

Shifting uncomfortably, I froze as her gaze landed on me. She picked up one of the shot glasses with a smile on her face and held it up to me. I tried not to glare at her. There was no way I could explain being a dick, especially toward Jay's sister.

The truth would not go over well, though. It wasn't even sitting well with me. Izzy had always been Jay's younger sister— his *much* younger sister. I'd known her for years and barely paid her any mind.

Until recently. Until something changed.

I zeroed in on her plump lips, glistening with a shiny coat of gloss, and cursed her existence for the dozenth time in the last six months. I snatched the shot from her hand, ignoring the sensation the brush of our fingers caused, and threw back the liquid.

"Guess he's not waiting for us." Adam chuckled before raising his glass around the table.

I narrowed my eyes at the idiot. We weren't fucking toasting or celebrating. Not after today.

Owen smirked at me from his spot on the other side of Izzy. Fuck. Did he know what was really bothering me? I wouldn't doubt it. He never missed anything. Well, except not realizing he slept with the Chief's daughter when he first started at the house. That whole situation was a mess. I shook my head as I spotted Chief Thompson heading toward our table. But it all worked out, I guess.

"Need another one?" Owen razzed, tipping his chin at my empty shot glass.

Maybe that was exactly what I needed.

If I drank more, maybe it would help me ignore Izzy and my growing attraction to her. An attraction I still didn't understand. She was almost twelve years younger than me. And Jay's baby sister. So no part of me could have an opinion on her shiny lips, intoxicating smell, or long hair that I wanted to tangle my fingers in. I just needed my dick to get on board and everything would be fine again.

The biggest problem was that, between Jay's wedding more than a month ago, the coed bachelor and bachelorette party before that, and—now that she had recently turned twenty-one— turning up at the bars we were at, avoiding her had become more difficult. Honestly, new guy's regrets or not, if I knew she was going to be here tonight, I would have stayed away.

It was hard to avoid anyone for long in our small town, but apparently, I needed to try harder.

Keeping my distance, and her out of my mind, would eventually solve the problem. Because there was no fucking way I was turning out like my father. Having a failed marriage on my resume was one step closer to being exactly like him, and I refused to add screwing someone over a decade younger than me to the list of similarities.

Izzy Mitchell was off limits. And after tonight, avoiding her was my only option.

Chapter Two

IZZY

"How about the coffee shop in town?" Nicole said and took a bite of her salad. "I saw a sign that they were hiring."

Two months into taking over the apartment from my sister Angie after she moved to a small town in Massachusetts, it was apparent I needed to get another job. I loved my position in medical billing at the hospital, but, as I was job sharing with Nicole, it was only part-time. She was the one who got me the job when her coworker quit a few months ago.

It was great that I could use my medical billing and coding degree, but the limited income wouldn't be enough for long. School loans I'd started paying off stacked up atop bills I hadn't even considered when I'd signed the lease on the apartment. I'd taken for granted the meals my mom cooked, and the internet provider I'd never needed to pay for. Gas and electric. Even a freaking water bill now.

Not that I would admit any of this to my parents or siblings. And have them tell me they told me so? Nope. I wanted—needed —to prove I could do this. That I was an independent adult now.

"I'll look into it." I took a bite of my own food before shaking my head. "But they probably want someone during the day. Maybe I'd be better waitressing somewhere."

Working at the hospital two to three days during the week, I needed a job I could do on nights and weekends. I was learning how to stretch a budget and was doing fine making ends meet, but I blew through my savings to provide the first and last month's rent when I leased the apartment. So now I had no cushion and little to no extra in that budget.

A second part-time job would give me a chance to build back up my savings and have a little extra. I hadn't even been out with friends in almost two weeks, doing my best to not spend anything that wasn't necessary. I missed that part of my life.

"Yeah, but you and I could always figure out a schedule if you needed to work somewhere else on specific days."

I appreciated how flexible Nicole was with our schedules. And, since she was in her last year of nursing school, my hope was that I could take over the billing position full time when she became a nurse.

"Thanks. I'll let you know if anything pans out. It's on my list this week to apply to a few places."

We finished our lunches and said our goodbyes on the sidewalk of the small eatery. I made my way back across the street to the hospital and through the lobby, waving at the ladies at the reception desk.

"Hey, Izzy," Paula called.

I turned toward her, and she waved me over. Maggie, one of the hospital's pediatric surgeons, was standing there. She was also the ex-wife of Logan Murray, one of the firefighters my brother Jay worked with. I'd known him for years, and we'd always coexisted easily, but recently, all he did was glare at me. Even his posture would change whenever I was close. He'd stiffen and act like if I touched him, he would burst into flames. For the life of me, I couldn't figure out why. Did I offend him at some point and not realize it?

"Are you still looking for a part-time job?" Paula asked as I stopped in front of the desk.

I nodded. "Yeah, why?"

"How are you with kids?" Maggie jumped in excitedly, a pleading look I didn't understand.

"Um..." I wasn't sure how to answer that. "Fine?"

I mean, I was a camp counselor as a teenager. And did my fair share of babysitting, too. But I really needed more context before I could truly answer that.

"I might have a job for you." She waved toward the coffee bar that sat in the corner of the lobby. "Let me buy you a coffee and I'll tell you about it. If you're interested, you can start as soon as tonight."

Tonight? Was she serious? This was already sounding too good to be true.

Once we were seated with our coffees, I listened to Maggie explain what amounted to a pretty amazing nanny gig. Before and after school hours, plus nights and weekends that wouldn't interfere with the hospital job. And I tried to hide my excitement, and relief, when she said how much they would pay me. It became clear very quickly that this was perfect for me.

"That sounds great." I smiled and nodded.

Her head tilted as her brow furrowed. Like she'd suddenly remembered a detail that had been lost in the excitement she'd originally felt when we started talking. "The schedule might be unpredictable at times. With our jobs, it's hard to predict when we'll be home." She took a deep breath before continuing. "So it might be difficult to plan personal time around the hours since they're not set."

It wasn't like I could afford to go out right now as it was, and I definitely didn't have a super active social life.

"Ideally, we want someone who can cook and clean up behind the kids. Maybe some light tidying around the house and the kids' laundry once a week."

I nodded again. "That's totally fine."

Did she not get I'd already said yes? Was she trying to talk me out of it now?

"And when we're on call, we'll expect you to stay over on those nights."

So they were going to pay me to sleep at their house? Again, I didn't see the drawback to any of this. I started to feel ridiculous as I continued to nod like a bobblehead doll, trying to convince her I understood.

"It's a lot of work, and the hours aren't consistent." She paused, searching my face. "I completely understand if you need some time to think about it."

"No!" I blurted before feeling my cheeks redden. I didn't want to risk her finding someone else. Not when I was sure this was the perfect fit for me. "I'm totally on board. I just moved out on my own, and the hospital job is part-time. I really need something else that's nights and weekends, so this is great."

"Okay. If you're sure."

"Totally."

"You can start this afternoon if you'd like." Her shoulders dropped, and her lips lifted into a wide smile. "I have extra booster seats you can leave in your car. And we have an extra vehicle you can use if you'd prefer that sometimes."

"Perfect." I listened intently as she explained what I would need to do this afternoon.

But when she mentioned I would be at Logan's house this evening, it finally dawned on me—I would need to deal with him a lot more. And not just in a personal setting, but as my new boss.

Somehow, in this whole conversation, the thought of working for the guy who didn't appear to like me very much never crossed my mind.

Rather than let that tank my excitement, I wondered if this was the perfect opportunity to show him who I really was and remedy whatever issue he had with me.

Chapter Three

LOGAN

I GRIPPED the steering wheel of the rig tightly as I maneuvered it down the street and back toward the firehouse. The fire was out, and other than wait for word from the investigators if this was arson or not, there wasn't anything else we could do.

We were pretty sure the result would come back as an intentionally set blaze. Secluded, uninhabited buildings, early morning hours, and no obvious cause were the hallmarks of our arsonist lately. If anything, at least he was predictable. The thing that worried us was the moment he decided he needed more of a thrill. When old barns and run-down buildings weren't enough.

Jesus. I flinched and prayed they'd catch him before that happened.

My phone vibrated in my pocket, and I bit back a groan. I

needed to deal with my ex-wife and our current childcare problem once I was back at the station.

Betty, our previous nanny, finally called it quits. Her increasing unreliability had been a constant frustration factor for us, but quitting on us last minute went way beyond our expectations. Alice and Nikki, our five-year-old twin girls, would probably throw a party once we told them the news, though. They were just as done with the older woman as we were. Guess this was the push we needed to find someone new.

In the seat next to me, Jay looked down at his phone. "Sarah says she can bring the girls home with her after school today. Then you can pick them up after your shift."

I nodded. "Thanks, man. That would be a huge help."

Jay's wife, Sarah, worked at the local elementary where my daughters went to school. On a couple of occasions when our childcare fell through, she was kind enough to bring them home and drop them off at the fire station. But those were times I was close to the end of my shift, and tonight I still had five more hours. By the time I would pick them up from Jay's house and get them home, it would be well after eight, and it was a school night. I would have little to no quality time with them, and they would be getting to sleep way past their bedtime.

It wasn't like I could leave my shift early. And although Maggie would take them if needed, I didn't want to give up the little time I had with them. It was the last night of my five-day stretch with them before they would go back to Maggie's after school tomorrow, so I had to make it work.

"What are you going to do about tomorrow morning?" Jay's voice cut through my thoughts.

I shrugged. "Not really sure. I can ask Dylan and Hattie."

For the umpteenth time, I attempted to brush away the worry about my current child care situation. Dylan, my neighbor and a detective with the Half Moon Lake Police Department, had been giving me crap for months about the multiple unreliable old ladies we'd hired over the last couple of years. Betty was just one of many, and a few weren't even unreliable—they just weren't good fits for a slew of reasons.

But Dylan was always willing to help if he could, and his girlfriend Hattie adored the twins too. Now that she was living there, I was hopeful between the two of them, one of them could watch my girls and then drop them at school. If I absolutely had to, I could come in late. But we were already short-staffed, so leaving the guys one man down didn't sit right with me if I could avoid it.

All of it was only a temporary fix. My mom and stepfather lived three hours north in Virginia, but they still worked. Asking them to come visit at the last minute was a dick move. We really needed to find a full-time, *reliable* nanny, and soon.

"I told you, you should ask Izzy."

That was definitely not happening. But I couldn't tell him that.

"She said something about looking for another part-time job."

Well, it wasn't going to be as my new nanny, that was for sure. My plan to avoid her had gone well over the last two weeks, and I hadn't run into her since that night at the bar. Seeing her every day wouldn't help diminish my growing attraction to her.

Luckily, I pulled up in front of the firehouse, and he jumped out before my lack of a response made things awkward. Jay stopped traffic, and I pulled the rig hard to the left before backing it up into the bay. Once I had it parked, we all climbed out and gathered our gear, checking it and getting it all set up for the next call.

My phone vibrated two more times in my pocket. I hadn't checked it since wrapping up at the fire we'd just dealt with. Pulling it out, I saw a string of texts from Maggie. When we'd talked this morning, she was hell-bent on finding a dependable nanny who wasn't seventy. At this point, I had to agree with her. Originally, the idea of a young nanny didn't sit well with me. My dad had cheated on my mom with someone almost twenty years

AJ RANNEY

younger than him. A woman who had, on occasion, babysat me when she was a teenager.

But I needed to remind myself our situations were totally different. I was only about to turn thirty-three, and I was no longer married. Not to mention, I would never get involved with the nanny anyway. You don't shit where you eat. Anyone with any sense knew that.

I clicked on the text notifications, pulling up my thread with Maggie.

> Maggie: I found the perfect nanny.
>
> Maggie: She's starting tonight.

Whoa. That was quick. How the hell did she find someone in only a day?

> Maggie: And you already know her, so it shouldn't be a problem.

Unease settled in my gut as I racked my brain for anybody I knew who might fit the bill as a nanny.

> Me: Who is it??

> Maggie: Izzy Mitchell

Fuck my life.

> Maggie: Perfect right? Money's tight and she could really use a part-time job. And she's good with kids. Perfect driving record and doesn't mind nights and weekends.
>
> Maggie: I can't believe Jay didn't suggest her to you.

I scrubbed a hand down my face. He did. Plenty of times. But

22

each time, I brushed it off. Because my fucking dick liked the chick way too much to be my nanny.

But what the hell could I say now? *No, we can't hire her because I get a hard-on every time she's around?* That would go over great. And then I'd have Jay up my ass asking why we didn't hire her. I wanted to have that conversation even less.

I wondered if I could turn this new development into an advantage. Maybe this was what I needed to squash my attraction to her. Seeing her with my girls would surely be the thing that would stop me from getting hard every time I was around her. If I thought Jay's little sister was off-limits, that title had nothing on my kids' nanny.

Chapter Four

IZZY

"Eighteen, nineteen, twenty. Ready or not, here I come." I removed my hands from my eyes and started my search for two little girls who were scarily good at this game. The last round I got a little worried when I couldn't find Nikki.

"Oh no. I think I finally lost them." This time I was catching on to what worked. I walked slowly, listening for the telltale giggles. "What should I do?"

I made my way through the great room and froze when I thought I heard something. Then jumped when the front door suddenly swung open.

"Daddy!" Both girls jumped up from behind the sofa, squirming their way out and rushing to the big man who stepped into the room.

He wasn't super tall, around six feet, but he was muscular, seeming to take up a room with his size. Validating the impression of power and strength, he scooped a girl up in each arm.

"Hey girlies." He greeted each with a kiss on their foreheads, and I nearly melted when they each tucked their heads into the crook of his shoulders. His gaze met mine, and the wide smile he wore a moment ago morphed into confusion before quickly turning into a scowl.

What was his problem with me? I couldn't imagine he was surprised by my presence. Surely Maggie told him I was starting tonight.

He focused back on his daughters, looking from one to the other. "You've had your showers?"

Alice nodded. "Yep, and brushed our teeth too."

"I made sure any homework I could see in their backpacks was done and made them dinner as well." Why did I feel the need to explain my worth to him? To make this grumpy man happy with me?

His gaze met mine again, and he gave me a clipped nod. "Thank you." Setting the girls down on the floor, he lowered his head between them and loudly whispered, "Why don't you go ahead up and pick out a book for me to read? I'll be up in a minute."

"Okay." They both replied in that same adorable tone, then turned and bounded toward me, almost knocking me over as they hugged me.

"You're the best, Izzy," Nikki said.

They called, "Goodnight," as they took off out of the room and up the stairs. Once the sound of their footsteps stopped, Logan turned his glare back on me and I fought the urge to shift on my feet.

"Did Maggie go over the schedule for the rest of the week with you?"

"Yes." I swallowed hard. "Tomorrow morning I'll be here at six thirty, drop off at school by eight thirty, and pick them up at three thirty. Then I'll take them to Maggie's. I'll be back here Thursday after school."

"Right." His jaw locked. "There's always a chance I get held up on a call, even after my shift is supposed to end, so I could be late." He crossed his arms across his wide chest. "That won't be a problem, will it?"

"No. Not at all." I attempted a smile, although I was sure the idea was foreign to him. "Whatever you need."

The tic was back in his jaw as he looked away and shoved his hands in his pockets. Apparently, that wasn't the right answer.

"You're welcome to use the SUV for drop off and pick up if you want."

I nodded. That would be a little easier than my two-door Hyundai. "Okay. Thanks." I started toward the door but froze suddenly, spinning to him once again. "Oh. The girls mentioned really wanting to do soccer. They said they usually couldn't do stuff like that, and I know it's a couple of weeks into the season, but I really don't think it'll be a big deal. They seem to have the basics."

His body sagged, and he let out a sigh. "The previous nanny wasn't very reliable, so that made it hard to commit."

That made sense. "Well, I'm happy to do whatever you need."

He shifted his weight, and I swore he groaned, but his lips were still pressed together tightly.

"Well, I'd better go." I turned slightly back toward the door. "See you tomorrow."

I took a deep breath once I was out on the sidewalk. The whole exchange was confusing. Angry wasn't right. More annoyed. But I couldn't understand why. Like our other exchanges, I struggled to pinpoint what made him so frustrated with me.

Maggie was beyond excited. Exuberant, really, that she'd found someone. She loved that I was someone she and Logan already knew and who the twins had actually met before. Someone who could drive and do all the things they needed. I assumed Logan would feel the same. I guess he just needed time to come around.

Whatever. Maybe whatever crawled up his ass would eventually crawl back out. His attitude wasn't my problem, and I would only need to deal with him a few times a week, since he and Maggie shared custody.

The schedule was a bit chaotic, but it made sense. It gave one parent a five-day stretch and then the following week, the other parent would have the longer stretch of time. But that meant some weeks I'd likely have to deal with him for five days straight.

Maybe I jumped into this too quickly and didn't completely think it through. My initial gut instincts rarely led me wrong, but this time I wasn't so sure.

LOGAN

The dirty fucking thoughts that flew through my mind when she said she'd do whatever I needed was shameful. What the fuck was wrong with me?

I'd hoped her being the nanny would fix my issue. Apparently not. It was like the minute I laid eyes on her long blonde curls, green eyes, and glistening lips, all the blood rushed south.

How the hell was this going to work? I couldn't go around sporting a semi the whole time she was here. Talk about a fucking cliche.

I had to hope it would get better. Because I didn't know how to get out of this arrangement. What could I possibly say? Even if

I came up with a dozen reasons she wasn't a good fit, Jay would be pissed if I fired his baby sister.

I trudged up the stairs and down the hallway before turning into the girls' room. They were sitting together on Nikki's bed, a book between the two of them. I chuckled, picking the book up and sitting down in its place. Both girls scooted closer, cuddling against me on each side. "Pete the Cat again?"

"You sing it good," Nikki said and scooted closer.

"Yeah, you do the bestest voices," Alice added. "Well, not as good as Izzy. She did so many voices."

I flinched at the mention of her name and swallowed uncomfortably before clearing my throat. "So you girls like Izzy?"

Both of their heads nodded.

"She was so much fun." Alice smiled up at me. "She let us listen to all the Taylor Swift songs in the car."

"Not the ones with bad words." Nikki shook her head. "So don't worry, Daddy."

"That's good." I needed more than that, though. I would give my girls whatever they wanted if I knew at the end of the day it was good for them. And I needed to know that Izzy would be good for them.

"We played soccer," Alice said, almost like she could read my mind.

"And she made spaghetti for dinner." Nikki bounced on the bed. "Like you make it. Not out of a can."

One of our many nannies we'd gone through in the last two years never cooked. The only meals she ever fed them was food she could warm up. Maggie and I had to pre-make meals and leave them for her to microwave.

"Was it good?" I asked, looking between them.

Their heads bobbed again. "So good."

I relaxed a bit.

Alice lowered her gaze to her lap. "We tried to be good, too, so we don't scare her away."

Tensing up all over again, I squeezed her shoulder. "Hey, that's not something you need to worry about, okay?"

"But if we're really good, she can be our nanny forever, right?" Nikki prodded next.

This was my fault. We'd gone through too many nannies over the last few years. But neither of them remembered the one who started with them and lasted almost three years. She was wonderful. But then she moved to Maryland to be closer to her grandkids. I couldn't blame her. Unfortunately, since then, it'd been one bad situation after another.

"Look, girls..." I hesitated, trying to find the right words. "Sometimes things don't last forever. You know, as you get older, you won't need nannies." I took a breath before continuing. "And I know you both really like Izzy, but if for some reason she can't be your nanny any longer, it has nothing to do with you or your behavior." They were fairly well behaved, so I could say that with confidence. But I wanted them to understand. "Okay?"

They shrugged like they were still convinced if they were really good, Izzy would stay. At that moment, I was determined to make this work. These girls deserved a reliable nanny who was good with them. Good for them. And if that was Izzy, then whatever issue I had would just need to shut the fuck up.

Because I wasn't messing this up.

Chapter Five

IZZY

Two hours had passed since I'd left Logan's house, and I still couldn't shake the feeling that maybe I made too quick of a decision when I jumped at Maggie's offer.

In my defense, I really didn't consider the fact that I would have to deal with how much Logan disliked me. Did I think Maggie hiring me would magically make him like me, when his actions proved over the last few months that he didn't? And why the heck did it bother me so much? I sat down on my bed and shot off a text to my sister, Angie.

> Me: So I might have done something crazy today...

> Angie: Is that supposed to surprise me?

I rolled my eyes. But I couldn't blame her for teasing me. Izzy doing crazy, impulsive things wasn't news.

> Me: Crazy, but now I'm second guessing it.

> Angie. Oh. That's different.

Her name flashed across my screen and I slid the answer button over to accept her call. "You didn't have to call."

"Eh. Wyatt's in Boston for meetings until tomorrow so I'm just sitting on the balcony listening to the ocean."

I smiled, knowing exactly what he was doing in Boston. I'd already gotten two pictures earlier today of engagement rings. I couldn't wait until he actually proposed. He made my sister so incredibly happy. The type of love they had—one for the fairy tale books—was what I hoped to have one day.

"Izzy, you there?"

"Yeah, sorry. Just thinking."

"Okay, so what happened and why are you regretting it?"

I filled her in on Maggie's job offer and my immediate jump at the opportunity. "The hours are perfect. I can still work at the hospital part-time, and seriously, the money they are willing to pay me is insane. I'll be able to pay off my debt and build my savings back up."

"So what's the problem? Do you not like the kids or something?"

"The girls are amazing. So sweet and fun. We played soccer in the backyard, and they helped me make dinner." I was almost surprised at how enjoyable I found the time I spent with them. I took a breath before admitting the real reason I was having second thoughts. "It's Logan. He obviously doesn't like me, and now I have to work for him."

She chuckled. "I've told you before, I think it's because he *does* like you, but doesn't *want* to like you. That's how Wyatt was when I first started working for him."

I scoffed. Our situations weren't anything alike. "I don't think that's it. He seems annoyed by my very presence."

"You want this job?"

I leaned back against my pillow and bent one knee, bringing it to my chest and tapping out a rhythm with my fingers. "Yes. It's perfect. And I think I could really enjoy it."

"Okay. So ignore the moody single dad and just do your job. He'll get over whatever his issue is eventually."

I blew out a harsh breath. Was she right?

It didn't matter. I shouldn't care so much that he didn't like me.

I wanted—no, I needed—this job. So the days I was there, I'd do my job and not worry about his not-so-pleasant disposition. Easy enough, right?

STANDING outside his front door the next morning, I squared my shoulders and knocked. I could do this. Ignore the big, growly man and his unpleasant attitude. No problem.

The door swung open and I stumbled back. Shocked wasn't a strong enough word for my reaction to what greeted me. Logan Murray was smiling. Not the biggest smile I'd ever seen, and I couldn't be sure it wasn't forced, but he wasn't sporting his normal scowl. I'd take it.

He stepped back and waved me in. "Come on in."

I followed him inside, shutting the door behind me. Inside the kitchen area that opened to a large great room, he stopped and spun toward me, crossing his arms over his heather gray T-shirt. The smile was mostly gone, but he wasn't scowling. Still a win so far.

"The girls are still sleeping. You need to get them up in the next twenty minutes."

I nodded. "Okay. Not a problem."

His jaw clenched, and I braced for the scowl I sensed coming.

AJ RANNEY

He took a visible deep breath in and his gaze locked intently on my face.

"They like you."

He said it like it was surprising. Did he think they weren't going to like me? Frankly, I'd yet to meet anyone, except for this man, who didn't like me.

"Okay..." I wasn't sure what kind of response he expected. "That's good."

He nodded. "Yes, it is. They've had a crappy go of nannies in the last couple of years." He shifted, almost uncomfortably.

I tilted my head, still not sure where he was going with this conversation or what I was supposed to say.

"I know you're young and..." He stopped, like he was searching for the right word. "Still figuring stuff out."

I was? What was I supposed to be figuring out? "I'm not—"

"I just want to prepare them if this is temporary for you."

Oh. *Oh.* I softened at the overprotective dad interrogation. I couldn't blame him for wanting to look out for his babies.

"Don't worry, papa bear." I smiled even though he was now back to scowling at me. "You all are stuck with me now."

The tic was back in his jaw, and the scowl deepened.

Note to self: Don't poke the bear.

Although teasing him was fun. Just an occasional small poke to keep things interesting.

Footsteps sounded on the stairs behind me, and I glanced over my shoulder as Nikki jumped from the second step from the bottom and they both raced past us into the kitchen.

Assuming our conversation was done, I turned to head after them.

"Izzy," Logan growled.

A shiver raced down my spine at the way he said my name. What. The. Hell? I shouldn't be turned on by the grumpy dad who definitely didn't seem to like me. I turned slowly, taking in his piercing gaze that anchored me to the spot. He closed the gap between us in three strides, and I had to tilt my head back to look up at him.

"I'm serious." His lips pressed together into a thin line.

"I'm aware." My lips twitched as I fought a smirk. Teasing him was truly a bad idea. Or maybe I wanted to hear him growl my name again. But I couldn't help it. I gave him my best cutesy smile and spun, leaving him standing there as I headed into the kitchen.

"Alright girls, what do you want for breakfast?"

"Pancakes?" Nikki asked a second before Alice piped up with, "Bacon?"

"How about both?"

They smiled, bouncing slightly on their stools that lined the other side of the island.

Logan stepped up behind them, wrapping an arm around each of them. "Have a good day at school." He pressed a kiss to each of their heads.

"Bye, Daddy," the twins chimed in unison.

He looked up and inclined his head to the front of the house. "Keys to the SUV and house are hanging by the door."

I nodded. "Got it."

He hesitated, staring at me, luckily without a scowl this time. Finally, he grabbed his duffel sitting by the entrance to the great room and threw the strap over his shoulder. One more quick glance our way and he was gone.

Thankfully, the twins would be with their mom for two days starting this afternoon. That would give me a two-day break from this confusing man who went from smiling to growling at me all in the span of fifteen minutes.

Chapter Six

IZZY

I LEANED my elbows on the kitchen island and swiped open the text thread with my sister.

> Angie: So any update on the Logan situation?

> Me: Not really. I've been at Maggie's since yesterday afternoon.

I wasn't telling her how my traitorous body responded to him when he growled my name. Or when he came so close, I had to remind myself to breathe.

> Angie: When do you see him again?

Me: Tomorrow night.

I couldn't help but wonder how things would end up being between us. Would he get used to me? Chat with me like Maggie did when she got home. It was hard to compare the two since I only had that one weird night and following morning at his house to compare anything to. But so far, he was growly and grumpy, while Maggie was friendly and chatty. The differences were drastic.

"Can we have three snacks?" Alice held up fruit snacks, a Little Debbie cake, and a bag of chips.

After that first night at Logan's, and now two at Maggie's, I had the evening routine down pretty well. The girls did their homework and then helped me make dinner, and they both did a great job. They would color or play with toys while I cleaned up, then they'd help me pack lunches before starting the bedtime stuff.

I shook my head. "Your mom said one healthy snack and two not-so-healthy snacks. So what fruit or vegetable do you want?"

"Okay." Alice's lips turned down in a pout. "Grapes, I guess."

Nikki turned toward the fridge and pulled out a yogurt smoothie. "Mom says these are healthy."

I nodded. "Yep, that's fine." Finished packing the lunches for tomorrow, they headed back to the table to resume their coloring. "Ten minutes and then we need to get ready for bed."

They both looked up with matching pouts. "Do we have to?" Nikki whined.

I raised a brow at them.

They giggled and went back to coloring while I finished cleaning up the kitchen. It didn't take long to go through the routine and get them both in bed once we were upstairs.

"One more, please?" Alice brought her hands up, pressing them together in a prayer pose.

I sighed. It was hard to tell either of them no. For the most part, they were extremely well-behaved. Although I sensed a little bit of orneriness bubbling below the surface at times.

I picked up one more book. "Just one more."

Alice launched forward, wrapping her arms around me. "You're the bestest nanny ever."

I chuckled.

"You do all the voices so good." Nikki smiled from her spot on her bed.

Alice pulled back, looking up at me with a huge smile. I swallowed hard. It'd only been a few days, but I was already loving this. Maybe it had something to do with someone actually needing me. Being able to take care of someone else.

I was the youngest of three siblings. The baby. Jay was six years older than me, Angie three. They never needed me, and my parents always went to one of them if they needed something. At least when Angie lived here, she appreciated my baking. I didn't even have that anymore.

I glanced back and forth between two identical faces, looking at me like I'd hung the moon, and picked up another book to read.

Chapter Seven

LOGAN

I shook my head at Zack, bopping his head to music only he could hear while cleaning the dishes. Sometimes his carefree happiness was welcomed, especially after a rough call. Other times, I found him flat-out annoying. But I couldn't deny the slight smile that lifted my lips.

The legs of the chair next to me scraped across the floor as Owen pulled it out and took the empty seat. "So, Izzy, huh?"

"What?" I coughed as I choked on the sip of coffee I'd just taken. I eyed him carefully, trying to figure out where he was going with his question.

"She's your new nanny?"

"Oh." Thank God. For a minute there, I thought he was going to call me out on being attracted to her. "Yeah."

His lips turned up into a smirk. "How's that working out for ya?"

"Fine." My voice came out a tad screechy, and I cleared it before adding, "Great. Girls really like her."

I couldn't tell him being so close to her the other morning was a special kind of torture. Between the scent of strawberries that invaded my senses and her large green eyes pulling me in, she was all I could think about after I left the house. I missed my girls when I got home, but the two-day break from all things Izzy was needed. I'd be lying if I said part of me wasn't looking forward to seeing her again tonight, though. I guess I liked the torture.

He chuckled and cocked a brow. "The guys are starting to take bets on how long it'll be before the apartment's love curse gets her."

My body tensed at the reminder. Starting with Owen, everyone who'd rented that apartment had fallen in love. Izzy recently took over the apartment from her sister Angie, so apparently that meant she was up next. Curses weren't real, I knew that. But that didn't change the fact that thinking about Izzy with some random guy sat like lead in my gut.

Luckily, Owen and I were interrupted by the alarms, pulling me out of my head and ending the conversation altogether.

Lake calls were some of the hardest we handled. Kids—hell, sometimes even adults—thought they could swim better than they actually could, and would go out farther than was allowed. It was a harsh reminder that there were limits for a reason.

I said a silent prayer as the information came through the radios and turned on the lights and siren before pulling the rig out of the bay. Jay rode next to me with Zack and Seth in the back. Since Adam had picked up an EMT shift today, he followed in the ambulance along with our resident paramedic, Kyle Williams.

Not surprisingly, Zack volunteered to rappel down the cliff face to the hiker who'd slipped and tumbled off a rock scramble. I had no problem letting the young guys do the crazy shit now. I was getting too old to rappel down fucking cliffs.

At least this call had a decent outcome, and the hiker walked away with what looked like a sprained ankle. Lucky guy.

Once back at the station, we all ended up back in the common area. Well, everyone except Seth. I eyed him as he walked past us toward the bunk room. He'd been here over a week now and had barely said more than a few words, and only when it was necessary. He wasn't only quiet, he actively avoided integrating himself into the house.

Firefighter teams were close-knit. We had to be to depend on each other like we did. You had to trust the guy behind you, or outside the structure you were working in, to have your back. I worried that Seth wasn't going to be the right fit. That his line of separation between him and us would end up causing problems.

"Just because you're married doesn't mean you're dead," Zack said.

I blinked and tuned back into the conversation. Was Zack still going on about the blonde bystander at the call?

Jay opened one eye from where he was stretched out on the sofa and peered over at Zack. "Maybe you should have gotten her number if you think she was that hot."

"Who said I didn't?"

We all groaned. Zack was the one who got baked goods delivered to the house as a thank you. The one who would smile and charm a crowd, or offer a hug to a distraught person on a call, or in a coffee shop. He was our very own golden retriever. We made jokes that we didn't need a dog, we had Zack.

I only had an hour left on my shift when the alarms rang again. Dammit. Fully involved fire meant I was likely going to be very late tonight.

Not only would it take longer to get under control, it was in a neighboring town, which meant longer travel times there and back.

"Jesus," Jay muttered as the large building, almost completely engulfed in flames, came into view.

"Yep, gonna be a long one." I voiced what I knew he was also thinking.

Taking cues from the company that arrived first, we took over handling the water supply for the large warehouse fire that required three different companies, and waited for additional orders. The next shift showed up in the tanker truck less than an hour later, but the fire was stubborn, keeping both of our shifts on site well past sunset. Chief Thompson and one of the other chiefs even called in the volunteer firefighters for our houses, and we still could have used more manpower. Fires like these were hell.

"Here." Seth held a bottle of water out toward me.

I cocked a brow as I took it from him.

"Don't want to be picking your heavy ass up off the ground, old man," he clipped.

"Don't worry about me." I smirked. "Pretty sure I'm in better shape than you."

With a chuckle, he opened his own bottle and chugged half the contents. I did the same. Staying hydrated was essential, and I appreciated his attempt at watching out for me. Hell, I think he said more words to me in that fifteen-second exchange than he had all week. Maybe he would eventually integrate into the team, he just needed time to get there.

I WAS UTTERLY EXHAUSTED when I finally parked my truck in the driveway and trudged to the side door. The house was quiet. I wasn't surprised the girls were asleep already with how late it was.

I set my bag down and looked around the kitchen. It was spotless. Did she make dinner? Because it didn't look like anyone was even in it today. I continued into the dimly lit great room, and my gaze landed on Izzy curled up on the couch.

I stepped closer until I was able to make out her features. Asleep on her stomach, her blonde hair framed her face, falling over her shoulder, and her long eyelashes lay flush against her cheeks. I groaned as I zeroed in on her bare lower back, clad in a short, tight crop top. The jeans she wore outlined the curve of her ass.

My dick throbbed uncomfortably in my pants and I closed my eyes, thinking about five different mundane things that only had a semi useful effect. I had to figure out how to do this. I had to make this work for my girls. I chuckled darkly to myself. Maybe today went horribly and they'd tell me she was awful.

Well now I was being an asshole. Izzy needed this job, I knew that. So for everyone's sake, I needed my dick to not like her so much.

Gritting my teeth, I grabbed the blanket off the back of the couch, avoiding looking at the beauty asleep in front of me. Quickly covering her up, I walked out of the room before my rebellious lower appendage took my gesture as a sign of encouragement.

Tomorrow we'd need to talk about the sleeping arrangements. I was so frustrated on Tuesday morning I forgot that was one of the things we needed to discuss. I had night shifts coming up in the next few weeks, and even shifts like today could run hours over. It made sense for her to have a setup in the guest room that she could use instead of sleeping on the couch.

Plus, I wasn't sure how many more of these late-night encounters I could take.

I glanced back over my shoulder, warring over if I should wake her or not. I decided against it. I doubted my ability to successfully hide my attraction to her after the day I had. Hard days like today made the nights of climbing into bed alone so much harder, and imagining her in my bed was too easy. That wasn't a road I was ready to go down.

Instead, I shot off a text letting her know I was home and she could go up to the guest room if she wanted, then retreated to my own room and shut the door. Cleaning up at the house before coming home was proving to be one of the best habits I'd gotten into. Because the last thing I needed was that image of her burned in my brain while I showered mere feet away from her.

And I wish I could say I successfully fell asleep without thoughts of her torturing me. But I'd be lying.

Chapter Eight

IZZY

I FELT disoriented as I stirred awake. Taking in my surroundings through blurry eyes, I shot up to sitting as it finally dawned on me I'd fallen asleep on Logan's couch. The great room was still fairly dark, so it wasn't time to wake the girls up yet. Grabbing my phone off the table in front of me, I clicked on the message from Logan.

> Logan: I'm home. Didn't want to wake you.
> Feel free to go up to the guest room. We'll talk
> in the morning.

The smell of coffee had me leaning forward to peer into the kitchen. Logan, in one of those tight as hell gray T-shirts, moved quietly around the kitchen. I stood and straightened my clothes before heading that way.

"Good morning," I croaked and then cleared the sleep from my voice.

He glanced over at me, his lips turning down in a frown, but quickly tore his gaze away, focusing back on adding creamer to his coffee. Well, this was going great already.

"You can use the guest room on nights I'm running late or when I have scheduled night shifts."

"Okay."

"If you wanted to leave a bag of stuff up there, that's fine."

I nodded. Not that he could see me because he still refused to look my way. His coffee was more than well-stirred, but for some reason, he kept staring at his mug and stirring it around and around.

Whatever. I was getting tired of trying to figure out his fifty shades of grumpy.

I walked forward and opened the cabinet next to where he stood, reaching up on tiptoes to grab one of the mugs. At only five-two, not much was reachable. But also, who put coffee mugs on the second and third shelves? Apparently, some six-foot musclehead named Logan.

Something between a groan and a growl hit my ears, and every muscle stiffened, locking me in place, my fingertips just brushing the handle of one of the mugs. In my periphery, Logan was locked on the bare skin of my stomach. My skin heated as I slowly lowered to the balls of my feet, my hand curled around the easiest mug to reach, and spun to face him. We were a foot apart, and when his gaze finally locked on mine, everything—or rather, some things—clicked together.

Logan Murray was looking at me like a man dying to taste forbidden fruit. Could my sister Angie be right? Was this why he was always so cranky around me?

His jaw locked. Footsteps bounding down the stairs like a

herd of elephants had him stepping back and focusing once more on his cup of coffee.

"Izzy," Alice exclaimed excitedly as she and Nikki entered the kitchen. "Can we make pancakes again?"

"Of course." I took a deep breath, trying unsuccessfully to shake off the need that coursed through my body at his heated gaze. "Nikki, you get the mixing bowl and spoons, and Alice, you can get the mix out of the pantry."

The pair went their separate ways and I turned toward the coffee pot, desperately needing my fix. I tried to ignore Logan's eyes on me. I could feel it, branding into my skin, and I didn't know what to make of it. Was I reading too much into this?

Probably. Because there was no way the sexy single dad noticed me in a way that was anything but Jay's annoying little sister. Right?

Stirring cream and sugar into my coffee, I stole another sideways glance at where he stood. He was sipping his coffee and not paying me any mind. Exactly. I totally read into the way he was looking at me earlier.

His head bent as his brows pulled together. I followed his gaze to where the girls were pulling out the stuff we needed.

"Are you really going to make pancakes?" he asked, still watching them.

"Yeah." I moved to the other side of the sink and opened the cabinet to grab a measuring cup. "We did it the last three mornings. It was fun."

He finally looked over at me. "Sure. If you like big messes."

I chuckled. "It's not that bad."

He cocked one eyebrow. "If you say so."

"Dad doesn't like messes."

"I don't like *cleaning* messes."

"Well, if you have time, you can help us, and then *I'll* clean up the mess," I offered.

The twins bounced excitedly, and a smile lifted Logan's lips.

Jesus. The grumpy single dad vibe was sexy, but it didn't hold a candle to the smile he was giving his daughters. So much adoration in that look.

He pushed away from the counter and stepped up to the island. "I have a few minutes."

Alice and Nikki beamed up at their dad as they took their spots on their stools, and I handed them the measuring cup. "Remember how much?"

They both nodded. "Two cups," Nikki said.

The first afternoon I picked them up, I was scared I wouldn't be able to tell them apart. Then it became obvious that Nikki refused to wear anything pink. Problem solved. Until neither of them wore something pink. Bridge for another day—hopefully after I'd already figured out a few more of their tells.

"Wait," Logan said, eyeing Nikki, who was ready to pour the mix into the measuring cup. "You let them do it?"

I shrugged. "Pretty much. I had to help whisk a bit, but they did almost all of it yesterday. They're really good at following directions."

"We did a good job." Alice smiled brightly. "And we got to help make quesadillas too."

He raised an eyebrow at me, and I smiled back. "They're great helpers."

Once the girls had all the ingredients in the bowl and whisked as much as they could, Logan stepped in and helped while I warmed up the griddle.

"I have to go now." Logan placed a kiss on the top of each girl's head. "Have a good day at school."

Their chorus of "Bye, daddy" was adorable as they climbed off their stools and headed toward me. Alice handed me the bowl, and as I took it from her, I stole a glance over at Logan. His jaw was tight, but at least he wasn't scowling at me.

His lips twitched when I shot him a smile, and he gave a slight shake of his head before turning and heading toward the door.

I focused back on my task, the girls chattering away about

funny shapes they wanted to try to make with the batter, but I couldn't stop thinking about the way Logan had looked at me earlier. Now that I'd had more time to think about it, it was actually pretty obvious.

Logan Murray found me desirable. And I liked that idea a bit too much.

Chapter Nine

LOGAN

IMAGES of her in that crop top took up space front and center in my mind most of the morning. So much so, I don't even remember getting to the station. And the way she moved around the kitchen, humming and talking with Nikki and Alice, I had to remind myself it had only been four days. She already acted completely at home in my house, and her energy was almost contagious.

I hated it. It would be so much easier if I found her annoying or unlikable in some way.

She had to have something that would turn me off. Maybe she chewed with her mouth open.

So far, everything had been quiet at the station. I wasn't sure if that was a blessing or a curse. Busy meant someone's day was going to suck. Quiet meant my mind had nothing else to focus on.

Worry bubbled up when my phone vibrated and I saw Izzy's name across the screen. It was almost nine a.m. She should have already dropped the girls off at school.

I hit the answer button and brought it to my ear. "Everything okay?"

"Well," she giggled. "Not really."

My spine stiffened.

"The back doors won't close."

"What?"

"Yeah. It's the weirdest thing. Alice got out and shut her door, but it wouldn't shut."

What did she mean it wouldn't shut? Before I could ask, she took a breath and continued.

"I sent the girls inside, and a mom came over to help me. She couldn't figure it out either." She giggled again, and I didn't think I was going to like what she was going to say next. "So I thought maybe if I looked at the way the other door shut, I could figure it out."

What was there to figure out? You just shut the damn door. I huffed out a breath, but before I could say anything, she continued again.

"But then I got that one stuck, too."

Was she kidding right now? "Stuck?"

"Yeah. The latchy thingy is stuck and it won't let the door close."

I gritted my teeth, at a complete loss as to what to say.

"I'll bring the guys and we'll head over." Because there was no way I was continuing this ludicrous conversation on the phone.

"Wait, like...you don't mean in the truck?"

What the fuck did she think we were coming in? A helicopter?

"Yes, Izzy. We'll come in the truck."

"But then the school will think I'm trouble."

54

"You are trouble," I blurted out.

A huff of indignation came through the line. "It's not my fault your SUV is weird."

I wasn't about to correct her and admit the hidden meaning behind my words.

"We'll be there in a few."

"K."

There was no way I could run some personal errand without the guys asking a million questions, and the last thing I needed was Jay there in case he picked up on my hidden attraction to his sister. So I gathered Adam and Zach under the guise of going to fill the truck.

"So, where are we going?" Adam asked once we were pulling out of the bay. "Cause the truck doesn't need gas."

Shit. I looked at the dash. A little less than three-quarters. Didn't matter. Wouldn't be able to hide where we were going, and why, forever.

"The elementary school."

"Why?" Adam looked over at me.

"Izzy's having a problem with the car."

Adam chuckled. "Ah, right. Izzy. The new smoking hot, totally off-limits nanny."

"Shut up, fucker." I attempted to force my body to relax. The last thing I needed was to give him any more ammo. "Can't leave her sitting at the school, now, can I? Jay would kick my ass."

"Think he's going to anyway," Adam muttered, and I sent him a glare.

Jesus. First, Owen and now Adam. Was I that obvious?

"How's it going with your student?" I fired back, giving him a taste of his own medicine.

"Fine," he gritted out.

That's what I thought. At least I shut him up.

"Where are we going?" Zack asked from the back, raising his voice to be heard over the roar of the engine.

"Need to swing by the elementary school," I hollered back. "Izzy had trouble with the car at drop-off."

I didn't miss Adam's smirk in my peripheral vision. Fucker.

Pulling into the lot, I cursed Izzy's existence once again. Maybe it was May and already in the seventies, but did that mean she couldn't wear actual clothes? After barely holding it together this morning, I had almost forgotten about the crop top she was wearing. Now I had Adam already suspecting something was up, so I had to school my reaction and force myself not to stare at the smooth tan skin of her stomach.

The SUV was parked in a spot near the entrance, and Izzy leaned against the back right side, engrossed in her phone. She looked up as I pulled the truck to a stop not far from her. We all climbed out and made our way the short distance to her.

"Ah, Izzy." Zack smiled, wrapping his arm over her shoulders. "How's my favorite Mitchell?"

A growl bubbled up my throat and tumbled out through my lips before I could stop it. Zack's eyes widened. Guess I had no choice but to address it. Besides, I was seeing red.

"Stop flirting, Stoer." I narrowed my eyes. "Or Jay will kick your ass."

He smirked, and I fought the urge to punch him.

"Nah, he knows I'm harmless." He tipped his chin at me. "You, on the other hand—"

"Don't," I warned. "Let's take care of the car situation so we can get back to the damn station. Not like we don't have jobs or anything."

I ignored Adam's snicker, but I didn't miss Izzy's eye roll. Zack still had his arm around her, and he continued to smirk at me like he knew he was riling me up.

Thankfully, Izzy moved away from Zack with a placating sigh and waved toward the open back door. "Like I said on the phone. It's stuck."

"Stuck?" Zack asked.

"Yup." She took two steps and swung the door shut. But it bounced back. "See."

"That's weird." Zack mimicked what she did, but slowly, as we all watched it not latch.

"Are the child locks on?" I asked, stepping forward and waving Zack out of the way. I didn't have them on because I trusted my girls not to open the doors until we were parked. Maybe Izzy didn't have the faith in them that I did?

But taking in Izzy's bewildered expression, I didn't think she had a clue what I was talking about. "Child locks?"

"Yeah." I pointed to the switch on the door. "This turns it on and off."

"Oh, that." She giggled. "Yeah, I tried flipping that on the other door, but then that one got stuck too."

I yanked the handle on the outside of the door hard until I saw the latch disengage, and then shut the door.

Izzy's mouth fell open in surprise. "Wait, how'd you do that?" She slammed her fists onto her hips. "I swear I tried the exact same thing."

"Brute force," I joked. "But I think it had something to do with the child locks."

"Not supposed to do that, I'm assuming?" Adam asked, stepping up next to me.

"No. Probably not. I'll need to take it to Randy at some point. Get it checked out."

"See?" Izzy smiled. "Totally wasn't my fault."

I raised an eyebrow and pointed to the door I just shut. "That one wasn't." I walked around the back of the car and pointed to the other open door. "This one was, though."

She shrugged. "How was I to know the switch thingy would get it stuck too?"

She shifted her weight, popping her hip out to the side. I tried not to track the movement. Tried not to let my gaze wander down to her bare belly. But I failed. And I was sure everyone saw it. Was wearing clothes that barely covered her stomach going to be a thing? Because it would be my downfall.

Adam cleared his throat, and I turned toward the open door. After closing that one, I headed back around the car and gave Izzy a nod. "See you tonight."

"If it's past ten, I'm going to take you up on the offer to stay in the guest room."

I swallowed and quickly nodded. "Okay." Somehow, the idea of her sleeping a room away made it feel even more real than sleeping downstairs in my living room.

Once she was back in the car, we climbed back in the truck and I pulled the rig out of the parking lot. The silence in the cab was deafening.

"Jay's so going to kick your ass, man," Zack spoke loudly from the back.

"He won't." I glanced in the rearview mirror. "Because nothing's going on." It was the truth. I was doing everything I could to not be attracted to her, and I sure as shit wasn't making any moves.

"Yeah, but how long do you think you can keep resisting that?" Adam side-eyed me. "Because the way you were looking at her, I'd say you don't have any chance of holding out much longer."

"Truth," Zack added. "I thought you were going to rip my arm off."

"Stop it." My knuckles turned white as I gripped the steering wheel tighter. "Nothing's going on, nor will be going on. Don't go starting shit."

"Dude, we won't need to." Adam smirked. "What we're telling you is if you look at her like you did just now in front of Jay, he's gonna think something's happening."

Fuck. Was I that obvious?

"Just openly flirt with her like I do. He'll think you're harmless, too."

Adam chuckled. "Or he'll kick your ass."

"Assholes," I mumbled.

I needed a better plan. Avoiding her was no longer an option, and I was obviously doing a shit job of covering up my attraction to her. How long could I possibly go without needing to be around both of them? Maybe if I admitted I was attracted to her and let him kick my ass it would remind me she was only twenty-one. His baby sister. My nanny.

Off—fucking—limits.

Chapter Ten

IZZY

I PULLED the car to a stop in the pick-up lane at the elementary school and put it in park. It would be at least another five minutes before they let out, so I glanced down at my phone, hesitating if I should tell my sister Angie anything or not. Would she tell me she told me so?

She was the one who said maybe Logan acted like an ass around me because he was into me. But if that were true, why did being attracted to me make him so annoyed? I didn't get it. Because he was friends with my brother?

I needed to talk to someone about it, though. At Jay's wedding back in March, I almost thought Logan was flirting with me at the bar. Until his demeanor changed and I talked myself out of it.

I sighed and switched over to my texts with Nicole instead. I needed someone to tell me I was being ridiculous, reading into things that weren't there. Nicole was the most levelheaded person I knew—well, besides my sister—but with this situation, I didn't need Angie adding things in my head.

> Me: I'm getting weird vibes from Logan.

> Nicole: Who?

> Me: Maggie's ex. The dad I'm nannying for now.

> Nicole: Oh. Weird like how?

> Me: One minute I think he's checking me out and then the next he looks pissed off.

> Nicole: Wait. I thought you said he found you annoying.

> Me: Well yeah. But now I'm getting the other vibes.

> Me: Just tell me I'm reading into things.

> Nicole. Do you want him to be checking you out?

> Nicole: Because if that's the case, maybe try a little subtle flirting and see if he responds. Then you'll know.

I sighed. Well, she wasn't going to be helpful. Somehow, the idea of the growly grumpy dad flirting was laughable.

The cars in front of me began moving as their children were loaded up and I pulled forward. Once Alice and Nikki climbed in the back seat and were buckled, I exited the school parking lot, my conversation with Nicole put on the back burner.

"Guess what?" I hoped they were as excited as I expected them to be about what I had to tell them.

"What?" They both responded in unison.

"Your mom got you both signed up for soccer."

"Really?" Nikki beamed, looking between me in the rearview to Alice sitting next to her.

"Yup. And your first practice is today." I still couldn't believe Maggie was able to pull it off. But she said she knew one of the coaches, so it made it easier to get them signed up and placed on a team quickly.

"That's so cool." Alice smiled, but just as quickly, her lips turned down in a frown. "But we don't have uniforms or anything."

"That's okay. Right now it's only practice. You can wear regular clothes."

"Okay." Her smile was back. "You're going to take us?"

I nodded. "Yup. We need to run home and get you both changed, and then head to the field."

They both beamed excitedly, and luckily it took us record time to change, grab a snack, and get to the field. It helped that they were motivated, and I didn't have to give instructions more than once. Not that they weren't good listeners, but like most five-year-olds, they needed constant reminders. Neither of them hesitated to run out and join the group of other kids their age once we got there, but Alice needed time to warm up to the idea of running after the ball. Nikki, on the other hand, didn't bat an eye and took off after it immediately.

I found a spot among the parents and waved to a few of the moms I recognized. Both girls were doing well, considering it was their first practice. Having practiced with them in the backyard after school this week, I could tell they would both pick up the sport easily. They thought it was cool that I played in high school. Honestly, I preferred softball over soccer, even though I played both. Wonder if either of them would be interested in that?

A woman in a blouse and dress slacks stepped over to where I stood. "Are you the Murray's new nanny?"

I nodded. "Yeah. I'm Izzy."

"I'm Susan. Rowan's mom." She pointed out her child.

We fell into easy small talk until the roar of a diesel engine had us both glancing toward the parking lot to see the fire truck pulling in. Did Logan go anywhere while on shift without that big thing?

Susan smiled, watching as the men jumped out and started making their way toward us. "I love that they all show up for them."

"Huh?" I turned back toward her and tilted my head.

"Like a few weeks ago at the fun run, they all came to cheer the girls on, not just Logan. I thought it was the sweetest thing. It's like they have a bunch of uncles."

I glanced back at the guys just as my brother waved. I sent him a wave back and then shifted my gaze to Logan. The tight, heather gray T-shirt clung to his broad shoulders and muscular chest. I didn't want to have an opinion, but I caught myself a few times wondering what it would be like to have those muscular arms wrapped around me.

His lips were in their normal firm line. At least he wasn't scowling. Before the guys made it all the way to us, a woman called out Logan's name and jogged over to him.

I was sure I made some kind of sound of disbelief when he smiled brightly at her. I get growly papa bear, but obviously, other women get friendly, flirty Logan. Which was fine. Why did I even care? I was tasked with watching his kids. I needed to stop imagining anything else.

The rest of the guys made it to us as Logan stayed a few feet behind, talking to the woman. I could make out a bit of their conversation involving fire safety week and promises to chat more about it over coffee. God, I hated that I felt jealous. I was being so ridiculous.

"They're pretty decent." My brother commented as we watched the kids run after the ball. "Kind of reminds me how you were. Never hesitated to go after the ball."

I nodded. "Yeah." I glanced down the line at Zack and Adam as Logan stepped up at the end. "New guy didn't come?"

"Seth?"

Right, that was his name. "Yeah."

"No." He shook his head. "He keeps to himself. Hasn't really taken to the group yet. I think we're a bit much for him." Nikki took her turn kicking the ball toward the goal and Jay tipped his head in that direction. "Logan was really happy you were able to do this." He chuckled. "He should have asked you about nannying months ago, like I suggested."

"What?"

"When they were having so many issues with the older lady being unreliable, I suggested he ask you. I think he felt bad firing her."

Zack made a noise, almost like a scoff, before he started coughing. "Sorry. I think a bug flew in my mouth or something."

Gross. Bugs in general didn't freak me out as long as they weren't on my skin or in my hair. And definitely not in my mouth.

Jay raised a brow at him. "You're acting strange, dude."

"More than my normal?" Zack smirked.

My brother sighed and crossed his arms over his chest, focusing back on the field. I tried to keep my gaze from roaming to Logan, but when I thought I caught him looking my way, I glanced back down the line.

And damn, I wished I hadn't. His lips lifted into a smile as he stared back at me, and my pulse took off into a sprint. If I thought his growliness was sexy, it held nothing to the smile that graced his face.

Or maybe I just enjoyed that it was directed at me this time. .

LOGAN

Watching my girls play soccer was the highlight of my week. The smiles they both wore as they chased the ball, the excitement they had the whole time, was nothing short of perfect. And it was all thanks to Izzy. Having someone who was willing and able to take them to practices and even games on weekends was huge.

Both girls barreled into me.

"Daddy, you came." Alice looked up.

"Did you see us?" Nikki added.

I smiled down at them. "I sure did. You guys did great."

The piercing tones of a call sounded from the truck, the muted alarms from the station a few blocks away following them a second later. Jay had already turned and was heading to the parking lot.

I squeezed both of my girls one last time. "Gotta go. See you at home." I gave Izzy a clipped nod and mouthed *thank you* before turning and jogging toward the truck.

Ten minutes later, when I pulled the rig up to a run down building engulfed in flames, I was praying it wasn't the fucking arsonist again. It had been almost two weeks since the last fire, but none of us were hopeful that meant he'd stopped.

Chief Thompson, Owen, and Seth were already on the scene. If both the chief and Owen were there, that meant they had the same concern. We grabbed our gear and piled out in front of the building. It used to be a small BBQ joint, but closed down over a year ago.

"Murray, Ricktor," the Chief boomed, "primary search. Mitchell and Stoer, take the new guy and get us a supply line going."

I nodded at Adam and we finished putting on our gear. I secured my mask in place and tipped my head toward the building, indicating Adam to take the lead. Having a slightly smaller build allowed him to squeeze easily in and out of tight spaces if needed. Luckily, the building was unoccupied, and we were able to get the fire out pretty quickly. The Chief didn't need to tell us he was calling this one in. We all saw the signs—forced entry at the back, multiple points of origin, inconsistent burn patterns. It was obvious. This was arson.

But before we could even get the scene cleaned up and secured, the tones for another call sounded. This one was a car accident involving multiple vehicles.

"Mckinley," the chief addressed Owen. "You go. I'll wait here for the agents."

Owen hesitated. None of us wanted to leave our chief here. What if the arsonist liked to hang around and watch his work?

Jay swirled his finger in the air, silently telling us to get in the truck. We had to trust the chief. And that MVC needed our quick response.

As we were pulling away, Owen and Seth following in one of the utility trucks, an unmarked cop car pulled up. Dylan got out, and I could feel everyone in the truck sharing my relief.

IT HAD BEEN ALMOST four hours since we left soccer practice, and to say I was exhausted was an understatement. My quick shower at the station probably did very little to scrub away the smell of the fire from earlier. Some calls made it harder to wash the day away before heading home, and I knew I'd still need another one before climbing into my bed tonight.

Walking into the house and hearing my girls laughing upstairs had me smiling and relaxing for the first time since I left them earlier at the field.

I set my stuff down and climbed the stairs two at a time, excited to see them before they went to bed. As I made it to the top, a vision in long blonde curls stepped from the room and collided into my chest with a squeal.

My hands shot out and gripped her shoulders. I swallowed thickly as she bent her head back to look up at me. Her eyes were wide, and her lips glistened as her mouth fell open. Her breasts pressed into my stomach, and the smell of strawberries engulfed me. Her skin felt so soft under my touch.

I couldn't stop myself from running my hands down her bare arms, eliciting a shiver from her as I did. A smirk pulled at my lips.

But then I blinked and stepped back. What the fuck was I doing? It didn't matter that she liked my touch as much as I liked touching her.

Nothing was happening between us. Period.

"Sorry," I gritted out. "Just coming up to say goodnight."

She nodded. "Yeah." The word came out breathy before she cleared her throat and continued. "I'll head out. Unless you need something else."

Oh. I needed something, for sure. But it wasn't anything I could actually have.

"I'm good." Desire to touch her again still coursed through my body as I forced words through my lips. "Thanks, Izzy."

She nodded and brushed past me. I stood frozen, not able to tear my gaze away quite yet. I wasn't sure what was worse, the crop top from yesterday or the one-piece tank top and tiny shorts thing she was wearing today.

I waited until she gathered her stuff and I heard the door click shut behind her before giving myself another moment to erase all things Izzy Mitchell from my mind and heading into the girls' room to say goodnight. They were both worn out and asleep by the time I left the room less than ten minutes later.

Tomorrow was my day off, and then the girls would be with Maggie for five days. I was almost grateful for another break from Izzy. Really I should've been fucking relieved, but I had to admit it was nice having her around. Even if my dick liked it a little bit too much.

Chapter Eleven

LOGAN

I STEPPED BACK onto the sidewalk after leaving the auto supply store and headed toward where I parked my truck. Having today off, and with the girls at Maggie's again until Thursday, I spent the day running errands. Grocery store, home improvement store for the parts to fix the upstairs sink, and then the parts I needed for my truck. It was easier to do things like this when I didn't have kids in tow. But even more so, it allowed me to spend more quality time with them if we didn't need to do a lot of tedious tasks.

I froze, hearing a familiar giggle, and looked across the street toward the park. Alice laughed as she ran around, kicking a soccer ball. I smiled when Nikki appeared, stealing the ball and running the opposite way. They were both pretty good, given they'd never played before.

Izzy chased Nikki, acting like she was going to steal the ball back. I stood, taking in the scene, debating going over. It wasn't that I didn't want to see my girls—I missed them during these long stretches—but after last week, it was clear the attraction I felt for Izzy was hard to ignore. Best thing I could do for both of us was continue to my truck.

But I couldn't make my feet move, nor could I tear my gaze away from the beautiful blonde. Her ass in capri leggings looked just as good as it did in tiny shorts. No surprise, she was wearing another crop top. How many half-shirts did she own?

Giving up on the battle, I made my way across the street, all the while trying to talk myself out of it.

"Daddy," Alice called when she spotted me, running my way.

I stepped onto the grass from the sidewalk and lifted her into my arms.

"Did you come to play with us?" Nikki asked once she and Izzy made their way over to us.

I smiled, trying to keep my gaze on my daughter and not let it drift over to Izzy. "I didn't know you guys were here, but I saw you from over there." I pointed across the street. "So yeah, I thought I'd come play."

I set Alice down and then lost the battle to not look over at Izzy. She stood with one foot on the ball, hands on her hips.

"Izzy's really good at soccer," Nikki said before adding, "She played in high school."

"Oh?" The corner of my mouth lifted into a smirk. "Better than me?"

"So much better."

Izzy chuckled at my daughter's response, and I raised an eyebrow before moving quickly toward her. She took off with the ball and I ran after her. Once I got close enough to steal the ball, she spun, not even slowing down, and headed back the other way.

Nikki ran down the opposite side of the field. "Pass it to me," she yelled to Izzy.

I smirked. Little traitor.

"Daddy, Daddy, get her, get her," Alice egged me on.

I was going to get her, alright. No, wait. Not like that. We were just playing a friendly game of soccer. But that didn't stop me from imagining ways it could be anything but.

Alice continued to encourage me as Nikki helped Izzy keep the ball from me. At least one of my children was on my side. Honestly, I wasn't surprised. Nikki was much more competitive than Alice.

Izzy slowed as I came up behind her, turning one way and then the other, preventing me from getting the ball away from her. She smiled over her shoulder at me, and the sight made my chest feel tight. Jesus, she was beautiful.

I crowded her space, and then, with a smirk, I wrapped my arms around her from the back. I tensed as my forearms brushed against the bare skin of her stomach, and my dick jumped to attention.

"I got her. Alice, get the ball."

Alice smiled and stole the ball, running down the field away from Nikki.

"You're cheating," Izzy yelled.

I lifted her off the ground and lowered my mouth to her ear. "And what are you gonna do about it?"

Her breath hitched, and a shiver raced through her. The smell of strawberries was so strong, my mouth so close to her neck, I had to fight the urge to move my lips lower and press against the skin there.

What the fuck was I thinking?

I blinked and let her go, dropping my hands to my sides and stepping back. She spun and we stood there, staring at each other for a heartbeat before she blinked and took off after the ball again.

I wasn't giving up that easily, though, and jumped right back in. Who knew practicing soccer could be so much fun? Sure, it was a game, but I shouldn't have been enjoying it—at least not in the way I was.

Being close to Izzy. Touching her. All of it was a very bad idea. So why did it make me so happy?

Chapter Twelve

IZZY

Talk about mixed signals. Yesterday at the park with Logan was so confusing. He didn't have any issues running around playing soccer with us, being playful and almost flirty. The way he so easily picked me up and whispered in my ear, and then went back to playing soccer like nothing happened... None of it seemed to affect him.

Me, on the other hand? I kept hoping he'd wrap his arms around me again. My stupid body responded to him in the most unfair ways. Did it not understand he wasn't interested? At least not in a way that made any sense.

Now he was here, and I was trying—very unsuccessfully—not to look over at where he and the rest of the guys from the firehouse sat. Could I not avoid him?

"You okay?" Nicole's voice pulled me from my thoughts.

I turned my gaze away from the group and picked up my cider. "Yeah, fine."

She'd texted after her nursing class tonight, asking if anyone wanted to meet for a drink. I'd just left Maggie's, with no plans for the evening, and now that I had a little extra money coming in, I could do stuff like this more often.

She glanced over at the guys. "Did you take my advice?"

"Advice?"

"Yeah. With Logan?"

"Oh." I shook my head. "No. I don't want to make things weird. I really like this job."

"But if he likes you too, aren't things going to continue to get weirder?"

"He doesn't. And I never said I did."

"Right. Okay."

"What's that supposed to mean?"

"You're in denial if you think you don't like that man. You've had the hots for him since Jay's wedding. But I digress."

I stole a quick look over, catching his gaze. He angled his beer my way before bringing it to his lips. Why did I find everything that man did to be either sexy or frustrating?

I smiled as two good-looking guys stepped up to our table and asked what we were drinking. Perfect, a distraction. Maybe this was exactly what I needed to get Logan out of my head. But I struggled to focus on anything the guys were saying, feeling Logan's gaze fixed on me.

Finally, I snuck a look back in his direction. His jaw was locked tight, and his lips formed a tight line as he stared back. I wasn't surprised. It was how he looked at me more often than not.

I sighed and excused myself to the bathroom. It wasn't Nicole's fault I wasn't really interested in the guys who were chatting us up, and she seemed to be, so I didn't want to ruin it for her.

Coming out of the bathroom, I turned down the corridor that led back to the bar area and almost bumped right into a familiar large wall of muscles. The hallway was narrow, and he took up nearly the whole width of it. I inclined my head back to look up at him.

"Having fun?" His words were friendly enough, but I could sense that underlying tone of annoyance he had around me lately.

I swallowed and shrugged. "Sure."

I was almost sure his eyes drifted down to the deep V of my shirt. But just as quickly, he pulled his gaze away and back to my face.

"Do you need a save?" He turned slightly and inclined his head toward the bar area.

I followed his gaze to Nicole looking back at me with a pleading look on her face. Oh shit. Maybe she wasn't that into the guy. I was so distracted, I must not have noticed.

"I can handle it." Having my big brother in the room would be a surefire way to shut them down if needed. Worked every time.

Logan huffed, and I raised an eyebrow. Did he not think I could?

"I have no doubt you can." He waved toward the table and turned, allowing me to brush past him.

I froze, the faint smell of smoke overwhelming me, reminding me of my father. Growing up with a firefighter dad, it was a smell I was familiar with. Sometimes, even after showering, he would smell of charred lumber and smoke. Most people would find the smell to be off-putting, but for me it was comforting.

With a deep breath in, I made my feet move, and I could feel his gaze remain steady on me as I made my way to Nicole.

"My brother and his friends want us to come join them." I inclined my head toward their table and grabbed my cider from in front of Nicole. "Sorry," I offered the guys with a quick shrug of my shoulders.

Nicole hopped off her stool and picked up her drink, following me toward my brother and the rest of his teammates.

"Those guys giving you issues?" Jay asked as I stepped up to their table.

I shook my head. "Nope. Not anymore."

Logan smiled as he took his stool across the table from me. Not exactly how I hoped this night would end. The idea of someone else—someone attainable and interested in me—making my body respond like it did with Logan was pretty appealing.

Too bad my body missed that memo.

Chapter Thirteen

LOGAN

Slow days at the house were the worst. A bunch of guys sitting around with way too much energy could be a recipe for disaster. Boredom and lack of an outlet had resulted in more than one argument through the years. None of those today, but the truck and all of our gear were now spotless.

A call toward the end of the shift ran over and made me late getting home. It was my first night back with Nikki and Alice since Saturday night, and I hated that I missed seeing them before bedtime. But I had three days off starting tomorrow, so that helped mitigate my frustration a bit.

I set my bag down in the foyer and climbed the stairs. After peeking in on them and verifying they were asleep, I gave them each a kiss before heading back downstairs.

I shouldn't feel excited to see Izzy, but I did. I had to admit it wasn't only my daughters I missed.

With a groan, I froze as I turned into the kitchen. She stood in front of the sink, washing dishes as she swayed to a beat. Her ass shook from side to side, the tiny shorts playing peekaboo. I closed my eyes, but all that did was conjure an image of me lifting her up onto the edge of the counter and devouring her mouth with mine.

I opened my eyes and cleared my throat, causing her to look over her shoulder at me.

"Just finishing these dishes from dinner." She smiled. "Then I'll be out of your way for the night."

I should be thankful. Her no longer in my space was what I wanted. What I needed. Right?

So why was I disappointed that she was leaving?

"There's a plate of chicken and green beans in the microwave." She turned back to her task. "If you want it. Wasn't sure if you ate at the house. I can put it away if not."

In my rush to get home in case the girls were still up, I'd left without eating dinner at the firehouse. "Thank you."

She nodded. "You're welcome."

I stepped up behind her, hitting a button on the microwave over her left shoulder. "Did you eat?"

"Yeah."

Grabbing the plate from the microwave and a fork from the drawer beside her left hip, I turned and leaned back against the counter. Izzy dried her hands and glanced up at me from under her lashes as I took a bite of the chicken.

"This is good." I swallowed as I stared at her. "Thank you, Izzy."

Her cheeks held a tinge of pink. She wore no makeup except whatever made her lips so shiny. Strands of blonde curls cascaded down over each of her breasts and I swallowed hard, pulling my gaze away from her chest and back to her face.

Regardless of my physical attraction to her and my increasingly failed attempts to control it, I couldn't deny she had been a huge asset to my family. I needed to make sure she knew that. "For everything."

She looked up at me, and I did my best to convey my sincerity and appreciation. The urge to talk to her, ask her about herself, struck me by surprise. But maybe that wouldn't be the worst idea. If I got to know her, if we became friends, I wouldn't have to fight so hard to resist being attracted to her.

A smile edged her lips, and her shoulders lifted in a slight shrug. "Just doing my job."

I cocked a brow at her. "Cooking for me is not your job. "

"Maybe not. But cooking for the girls is. You just got lucky that we had leftovers."

I chuckled and forked the last bit of green beans into my mouth. "Well, I appreciate it." I brushed past her and rinsed my plate before putting it in the dishwasher.

"So you have off until Monday?"

I turned to face her, leaning back against the sink. "Yeah. I'm assuming Maggie's PA sent you our schedules?"

"She did. It's very organized. I was impressed." She folded her arms across her chest, making it hard to not glance down at her tits rising up into the scoop of her tank. "You have the girls until Saturday night. I won't be needed until Monday morning at Maggie's house."

I nodded. "Yeah, and not sure if Maggie mentioned it, but switching houses is fairly new. We started trying it in January."

She shook her head. "I don't understand. What did you guys do before?"

"It's called nesting." I crossed one ankle over the other. "We wanted to make sure both Nikki and Alice were comfortable when we first separated, and we both work weird hours, so it kind of made sense."

Taking in her furrowed brows, I gathered she still didn't get it.

"Basically, the parents move, not the kids. I built a studio apartment over the garage for myself. Maggie got herself a condo. We took turns being here in the house with the girls."

"Oh." She smiled. "I guess that makes sense. So why did you guys decide not to continue it?"

I shifted uncomfortably, not wanting Izzy to think badly of Maggie. We were in a good place and co-parented well as a team. And while it might've been her idea to stop nesting, her reasoning made sense.

"Maggie started seeing someone, and once she thought it was getting serious, she decided it was best to move forward with our daughters going back and forth between our homes. I agreed. Nesting was great to help them transition, but it's not a forever thing."

She nodded. "The girls seem to be doing okay with it."

"Yeah, they've adjusted well."

"Why did you guys get divorced?"

I flinched. Jesus. I wasn't expecting that. She didn't have a filter, that was for sure.

"What?" she asked with a shrug as she studied me. "I'm just curious."

"Ever heard of what curiosity did to the cat?"

"But I'm not a cat." Her lips lifted into a wide smile.

I fought the urge to laugh at her ridiculousness. But I didn't have anything to hide, and I wouldn't lie to her either.

"We were young when we got married, both of us focused mainly on our careers. Looking back, we should have tried harder to make each other a priority. And I don't think either of us realized how much having kids would test our marriage. Neither of us wanted our kids to experience what we did as kids—parents who fought all the time."

"I can't imagine you two fighting. I mean, you're both so patient with the girls."

I shrugged. "We're better apart than together."

Silence engulfed us as she thought about what I said.

"Were they good for you tonight?" I'd yet to get any bad reports, and they were usually well behaved, but her statement about us being patient with them made me wonder if they weren't good with her.

"They're always good, and they were adorable tonight." She chuckled. "Got so excited when I mentioned my dad was a fire-fighter too."

"Yeah?" I could picture them thinking that was a cool thing to have in common. "I always worry they'll look back and only remember all the nights I wasn't home in time to say goodnight." Why did I even admit that to her? Maybe because I thought she'd understand?

"I don't think they will." Her head cocked to the side. "I remember my dad being the one who came to most of my school stuff because he would have random days off during the week."

"What does, or did, your mom do?" I wanted to know more about her, and it surprised me that this was something I didn't know. Jay's dad being a firefighter was memorable, but if he ever mentioned what his mom did, I couldn't recall.

"Mom works as a receptionist in a vet's office." She tucked a strand of hair behind her ear. "She's been there for like fifteen years. No plans to retire anytime soon. Says she'll go crazy stuck home with my father all the time." A smile tugged at her lips.

She glanced around the kitchen, almost like she was trying to find something else to talk about. And as much as I wanted that too, it was getting late. The girls would likely have me up before seven. She must have read my mind, because before I could say anything, she said, "I'd better get going."

I glanced at my watch. "Yeah. It's getting late."

She smirked. "Maybe for you, old man. I'm grabbing drinks with friends." She grabbed her phone and small wallet off the island. "I'll see you Tuesday morning."

I locked my jaw tight as she turned to leave. Why did I hate the idea of her going to a bar, where guys would be competing for her attention? Like the two guys a few nights ago. Would she go home with one of them? The thought had me seeing red.

But that didn't matter. There was nothing I could do about it. Izzy wasn't mine, and never could be.

Chapter Fourteen

IZZY

WHY DID I think going out for drinks last night was a good idea? Especially knowing I had to work at the hospital today. Maybe I should have skipped the shots.

My head throbbed and I popped two over-the-counter pain relievers in my mouth, swallowing them with a sip of my coffee. After stashing my bag under my desk, I pulled up my email and began sorting through the messages, making sure I didn't miss anything important since I hadn't been here since Tuesday.

The morning went by quickly as I submitted claims and prepared invoices to go out. My phone vibrated in my pocket as I made my way down to the cafeteria. I'd been good about packing lunches, but today I was barely functional after getting out of bed, so it looked like it was a soup and salad type of day. Once I was seated with my food, I pulled my phone out and clicked on the notification from Nicole.

> Nicole: Any update?

> Me: ...

> Nicole: With the sexy single dad? I totally caught him looking at you at the bar on Tuesday.

I rolled my eyes. Was he not allowed to look at me? Now I had Nicole reading into things that weren't there.

> Me: You're ridiculous. He's been totally normal. Totally friendly and shit.

Mostly. I wasn't going to tell her that there was a weird moment after I came out of the bathroom at the bar. When I swore his gaze drifted down to stare at my breasts.

> Nicole: If you say so.

"Hey, Izzy."

I looked up at the sound of Maggie's voice. "Hi."

She waved to the open seat across from me. "Mind if I join you?"

"Sure."

She pulled out the chair and sat down. "Did you have any questions about the schedule my PA sent you?"

I shook my head. "Nope. It's pretty straightforward." I appreciated the organization, having the whole month, plus next month, laid out.

"Perfect." She paused, taking a bite of her salad. After a moment, she asked, "And the hours won't interfere with here, will they?"

"Nah. I worked it out with Nicole." Luckily, we had the option to work out the hours among ourselves, and it helped that we were both flexible.

"Okay. Great." She smiled brightly. "Alice and Nikki have talked nonstop about you. Wish we could have made this happen months ago."

I chuckled. "Yeah, but nobody wants to fire an old lady."

"Um, I did. Multiple times." She scoffed. "Even Logan was ready to give her the boot back in March."

Huh. I tilted my head. "So why didn't you?"

She shrugged. "We had trouble finding someone else we both agreed on."

Now I was officially confused. Because that wasn't lining up with what my brother had said. "Jay said he mentioned me as an option once or twice over the last few months."

She paused, her fork halfway to her mouth, and stared at me, blinking. *Shit.* Maybe Logan was the issue, and for whatever reason, he didn't want to hire me. That idea didn't dawn on me until now as Maggie's surprised expression morphed to annoyance.

"That man, I swear." She shook her head.

I raised a brow and she waved me off. "Water under the bridge now. Whatever his issue, he must have gotten over it. He admitted you're great with the twins and seems happy with the decision."

I wasn't sure I was completely following the conversation. But my takeaway: He never mentioned Jay's suggestion. So maybe he did have some issue with me. Maggie was right, though—whatever it was, he apparently let it go. Last night he was perfectly fine. I didn't even get a growl.

Not sure why I felt disappointed about that.

"And you're good with the occasional overnights, too?" She glanced up at me as she took another bite of her food and swallowed. "I know we talked about this briefly already, just making sure."

I nodded. "Yeah, no problem at all."

I didn't want to sound desperate, but man, I needed the type of hours and money these people were offering me.

Her lips lifted into a wide smile. "You're a godsend. I wasn't sure we'd ever find someone that was both great with kids and could handle our schedules."

"And they do summer camp?" We'd talked about a few options the other day, but not since.

"Right now we have them enrolled in the every day program. But like I said earlier in the week, we could take it down to three days a week if you wanted two full days. Just keep in mind, we'd still need the late nights, occasional overnights, and weekends."

I let that information sink in. "When should I let you know by?"

"Probably in the next week or so."

"Okay."

We chatted about the summer camp until an alarm sounded on her phone.

"Gotta get back upstairs." She gathered her almost empty salad container and smiled at me. "I'll see you Monday morning."

I nodded, and my phone vibrated on the table in front of me as Maggie walked away. A mix of surprise and excitement coursed through me as a text from Logan appeared in the notifications.

> Logan: Had to pick Nikki up from school.
> She's sick. We can't find Benny. Any ideas?

The small white stuffed rabbit was a must at bedtime. I'd learned that pretty quickly after that first night when Logan came home late. She definitely had it with her last night, didn't she? God. I hope we didn't leave it at Maggie's.

> Me: Pretty sure she had it last night. Check
> behind the bed? Or maybe tangled in the
> blankets at the foot of her bed. That's where I
> found it the other night.

I waited a moment, and after no response, I finished my food and cleaned up before heading back to my desk to finish what I needed to get done today. After what felt like the longest three hours ever, I finally walked to my car. I still hadn't gotten a response from Logan, so once I got in the driver's seat, I shot off a text.

> Me: Did you find it?

> Logan: Oh. Yes. Sorry.

> Me: I can swing by the school and grab Alice so you don't have to take Nikki out if you want.

I didn't want to overstep, but I would offer to help anyone else I knew. It was who I was.

> Logan: Really? You wouldn't mind? She's finally resting. If I don't have to put her back in the car that would be great.

> Me: I don't mind at all. Anything you need? Soup, medicine, popsicles?

I didn't know what she was sick with, but based on my own experiences growing up, I assumed those were the must-haves.

> Logan: I think I'm set. Thank you for offering.

> Me: No problem. Leaving the hospital now and heading to the school. See you soon.

Luckily, I kept the booster seats Maggie gave me on that first day in my car. I didn't want to be out somewhere and need them. It didn't take long to pick up Alice and get to the house.

It was quiet when we walked in the front door. I dropped Alice's book bag in the foyer, and we made our way past the stairs before turning into the great room. Logan lay on the couch with his forearm over his eyes. Hopefully he wasn't getting sick, too.

"Da—" Alice started, but stopped when I put a finger over my mouth.

I leaned down toward her when Logan didn't stir, and whispered, "Let's let him rest. Want to help me make chicken noodle soup?"

She nodded, her head bobbing with excitement. We quietly made our way into the kitchen, and I gave her a list of ingredients to get out.

"I'm going to peek in on your sister. I'll be right back."

After checking on Nikki and confirming she was sleeping and only felt slightly warm, I went back down to the kitchen. Alice got the vegetables out, I cut them while the chicken cooked, and then we added everything to the pot with chicken broth, some seasonings, and noodles. I put the soup on simmer and asked Alice about her day.

As I listened intently to Alice talk, I caught movement at the entry of the kitchen.

Nikki rubbed her eyes sleepily. "Izzy?" She glanced around. "Where's Dad?"

I pointed toward the great room. "He's resting on the couch." I stepped toward her and placed the back of my hand on her forehead. Still slightly warm, but not hot. "How are you feeling?"

"My head hurts and my throat feels weird."

She flinched as she swallowed. Hopefully it wasn't strep. I got that crap a lot growing up.

"Want to try a little bit of chicken noodle soup when it's done?"

She nodded. "Yeah."

Rustling from the couch made our heads swivel that way. Logan sat up and glanced over at us before running a hand over his face. He stood and headed toward us. "What time is it?"

"A little after five."

"Shit."

"Dad," Alice scolded.

"Sorry. Shoot." His gaze found mine. "Why didn't you wake me?"

"Figured you were tired and needed to rest." I shrugged. "Alice and I made chicken noodle soup."

He looked from the pot on the stove back to me, before his gaze ran over Alice and finally landed on Nikki. He repeated the motion I did a few minutes before, checking to see if she felt warm.

"Throat still hurting?"

"A little," she replied.

"I hope it's not strep again." He glanced up at me. "She's had it twice already this year."

I flinched. That sucked.

"Thank you." His sincere gaze trained on me made me squirm.

I couldn't explain it. Maybe it was because he was so much more serious than guys I'd been around, but when he looked at me with so much intensity and appreciation, I had no clue what to say.

"No problem." I smiled, still feeling a bit awkward as he stared at me. "Well, I'd better get going. Soup is probably done."

"Wait." Alice's big blue eyes zeroed in on me. "You have to try some soup with us. You helped make it."

I chuckled. But before I could respond, Logan's deep voice reverberated around the kitchen. "You should stay."

I whipped my head up, my skin warming from his gaze. Jesus. What was wrong with me?

"Unless you have plans again." His voice sounded gruff now. Like he was forcing the words out. His lips started to form a scowl.

"No. No plans." I shook my head. I didn't understand my need to please him. To want him to look at me with appreciation. No one ever needed me, and I'd be lying if I said I wasn't enjoying the way his gaze was begging me to say yes. "I can stay for a bit."

My breath caught, and my knees literally felt weak as a smile lifted his lips. Maybe staying wasn't the best idea. The last thing I needed was to be crushing on my boss. I wanted him to like me, and not look at me with annoyance anymore, but vying for his attention had bad idea written all over it.

I turned away from him, needing a moment to shake him off, and started to pull bowls down from the cabinet. But I froze mid-reach when I felt him step up behind me. With a deep breath in, I lowered my hands and spun slowly to face him.

"Here, let me help," he said, taking the bowls from my hands.

Our fingers brushed, sending tiny pricks of sensation coursing through me. Damn my body for reacting to this man. A man I could never have. He set the bowls down on the counter next to him and grabbed the top one, holding it out for me to scoop soup into. I grabbed a ladle out of the drawer and filled the first bowl. He handed each girl a bowl and then carried the last two over to the table.

I took the seat across the table from Logan, next to Alice, and Nikki sat next to her dad. She slowly started looking and sounding much better while we ate. The girls talked nonstop, and I couldn't help but smile at the way they finished each other's sentences. I tried to ignore the times I felt Logan's eyes on me. It did neither of us any good to read into his actions.

I was his nanny. His teammate's little sister. There was nothing more to it. If I repeated it enough, maybe my body would take the hint.

Chapter Fifteen

LOGAN

I HUGGED both girls one last time and then waved as they made their way up the sidewalk to the front entrance of Maggie's condo. Nikki was much better today. No fever and not complaining about a sore throat. Which was good, because if she kept getting strep, eventually they might suggest we get her tonsils removed.

Maggie held up one finger, signaling me to wait as she ushered our kids inside. She headed down the sidewalk with one of her looks that told me I was about to get an earful.

Shit. I couldn't think of a reason why she'd be upset with me. But I had a feeling I was about to find out.

"Why didn't you tell me Jay suggested we hire Izzy months ago?"

I swallowed. How was I supposed to answer that?

"I get you're still hung up over what your father did, but it's not like you'd ever consider hooking up with your friend's sister."

I grabbed the back of my neck and looked at the ground between us. This conversation was a minefield of epic proportions.

"Wait." She gasped.

I glanced back up at her, taking in her wide eyes.

"Oh my God." Her mouth fell open. "You like her."

I shook my head. No. My dick liked her. I found her irritating. Well, not her, but the way I lost all sense whenever she was around. Like last night—inviting her to stay and catching myself staring at her multiple times throughout the evening.

Maggie chuckled, and I narrowed my eyes at her. I wasn't doing this with my ex-wife. She might think the situation was funny, but I didn't.

She schooled her features. "Logan, you're single. If you like Izzy, ask her out. It's not the same as your father. You're no longer married."

I crossed my arms over my chest. That wasn't happening, and now I had even more of a reason to make sure it didn't. "She's amazing with the girls, and reliable, and everything we've wanted in a nanny. I'm not going to screw that up by sleeping with her."

Maggie rolled her eyes. "You've had one serious relationship, and then you married her. I'm sure the next woman you end up dating will end up being something serious. I don't think you're capable of casual."

"I'm starting to understand why Dylan says we have a strange relationship." Only my ex-wife would feel it necessary to give me dating advice.

She shrugged. "We were friends long before we were anything more, and we've known each other more than fifteen years at this point."

"I'm not dating Izzy," I said, trying to convince myself more than her. Because it was only physical attraction I felt toward her,

I was sure. Almost. Regardless, I wasn't willing to screw up the situation with the girls. "So just drop it."

"Fine." She sighed. "There's one more thing I wanted to talk to you about."

I cocked a brow.

"Jesse and I have started talking about moving in together." I liked the guy she'd been dating since the end of last year, and honestly, I wasn't surprised by this development in their relationship. "Probably not until the end of summer, though."

I nodded. "I'm assuming you're moving into his house?" It made the most sense since he had the extra space and Maggie only had a two-bedroom condo. But it was one town over, which meant a different school district.

"Yeah." As if she could read my mind she added, "But the girls would stay at the school they're at now. I'm fine with the extra drive, and I'll mention it to Izzy as well. I don't think she'll mind."

"Jesse's a good guy." A smile lifted my lips. "I'm happy for you."

"Thank you. You know I want the same for you, too."

Jesus. Not this again. I was not dating Izzy Mitchell.

"Just consider what I said. You. Are. Not. Your. Father." She sent me a sympathetic look and sighed, knowing I wasn't getting into this with her again.

I wasn't even sure my father's behavior was my biggest reason for not getting involved with Izzy. I'd mostly dealt with his betrayal, although I still refused to touch the trust fund he set up for me. I had it set up for the girls if, given my career choice, anything ever happened to me. But I didn't need nor want his money.

Izzy had become a valuable asset to us, and I didn't want to mess that up. She also deserved someone close to her age who didn't have the type of responsibilities I did. I doubted she'd want something serious with a divorced single dad who had an unpredictable schedule at a job fraught with its own risks.

"I'll drop the girls back off Monday evening."

Maggie's voice pulled me from my thoughts and I nodded.

A few moments later, I was back in my truck. I wanted to make a stop before I went back home. They'd declared the fire at the old BBQ joint arson, sure it was our guy—or woman, but typically eighty to ninety percent of arson cases involved male perpetrators—but they hadn't been able to find anything that would lead us to a suspect yet. The places are always run down and vacant. No security footage, and so far they'd been able to start the fire without anyone seeing. All we knew was they were using kerosene as the accelerant, and matches to start it.

Arson is one of the hardest crimes to solve. The fire itself destroys most evidence left behind. The chance I would find anything the investigators hadn't was unlikely, but I couldn't sit around and wait for another one to start. And something was nagging me. Up until now, each location had a broken window, which investigators determined was where the arsonist threw the lit matches into the building. But this one didn't have that.

Why? It didn't make sense. Did he light the matches while he was standing inside the building this time? Or throw them in from outside the back door? He could have technically done that at any of the other fires, but didn't. What made this place different? And this was the only one not set in the early morning hours. It almost felt unplanned.

I parked my truck and grabbed a flashlight before getting out. It wasn't totally dark, the sun making its final descent below the horizon, but inside the building would be dark. It had been more than a week, and the investigators were done with the scene.

I had no clue what the fuck I was doing. What I thought I would find. I gently sifted through the interior remains, looking for anything that might help. A loud clang sounded from outside the back of the building, but when I stepped through the back door, there was no sign of a person.

Movement fifty feet away caught my eye as what looked like a person moved along the tree line. As I hurried that way, my flashlight shone on something red lying on the ground only ten feet from the back of the building. A matchbook. I picked it up with one gloved hand, turning it over. It wasn't charred. So it wasn't in the building. Did whoever I saw a moment ago drop it?

I pulled out my phone and dialed Dylan. He was not going to like what I had to say.

"What's up?" he asked the moment the call connected.

"I need a favor."

"Dude, you have a nanny now." He chuckled. "One that isn't eighty."

I rolled my eyes. "Not that type of favor. Girls are with Maggie. I'm at the BBQ place, the one that burned down."

"Why?"

"Because I'm tired of rushing into burning buildings that are being set intentionally."

He sighed. "Not your job, man. You gotta let the fire investigators take care of it."

"Yeah, well, they're not." I huffed out a breath. "Need you to get Violet over here. I found something. I think he's coming back to the scenes after the fact."

"I'll call Violet on my way over."

Hopefully, his tech could pull prints from the matchbook. I looked down, turning it over again. The front read *Taylor and Sons Plumbing*. Or maybe this company could lead us to a suspect.

Chapter Sixteen

IZZY

THE WEEKEND WENT by entirely too fast, even though I didn't do much besides cleaning and grocery shopping. Not exactly how I imagined twenty-one to be. At least I was going out tonight for Nicole's birthday.

"All done?" I asked Alice.

She nodded. "Your turn."

I took over stirring the cookie dough mixture. They wanted to make chocolate chip cookies before their mom got home, stating it was her favorite treat. And as it was one of my favorite things to do, I'd use any excuse to bake.

They took turns scooping balls of dough onto the cookie sheet before I slid it into the oven. The timer went off, and my phone chimed from the counter as I was pulling the cookies back out. I picked it up and clicked on the text from Maggie.

> Maggie: Would you mind getting the girls packed up and driving them over to Logan's? I've got an emergency surgery.

Any other day I would have taken them to Logan's after school, but school was closed today for a teacher in-service day. Maggie and I already discussed the possibility of me taking them to Logan's if she was running late. And I couldn't even bring myself to be upset about the change in plans. The idea of seeing him again shouldn't excite me so much. But it did. I typed out a response to Maggie.

> Me: Of course.

"Hey, girls." I waited until they appeared at the entrance to the kitchen. "Can you run upstairs and get your stuff for your dad's? Your mom's going to be late tonight."

They both nodded and took off running. Apparently, the change in plans didn't bother them either. But they were always excited to see Logan. He's their dad. What was my excuse?

Shaking that thought from my brain, I busied myself in the kitchen separating the cookies into two containers. Alice agreed to leave some for Maggie and take some to their dad, too. That was only fair.

When I pulled down the driveway that ran along the side of Logan's house, my gaze landed on Logan under the hood of his truck in front of the detached garage. My breathing increased as I took in his shirtless back, his jeans hanging low on his hips.

Jesus. The amount of muscles on him was insane.

I pulled my bottom lip between my teeth as he turned to face us, struggling to look at anything but his wide shoulders and how defined his chest and abs were. My core throbbed. Why did he have to be so freaking sexy?

The girls jumped out and grabbed their bags before running toward him. I took a deep breath and grabbed the container of cookies from the passenger seat. Not like I could sit in the car any longer and drool over the man.

Having gotten hugs and hellos, two identical heads, with their dark hair pulled back in matching ponytails, blew past me on their way to the side door of the house. "Bye, Izzy," they both said before disappearing inside.

It looked like I was giving the sexy single dad his cookies because his kids forgot all about them. I stopped a few feet from him and thrust the container out toward him. "Here."

He cocked a brow, glancing down at the cookies and then back up to my face.

"They're cookies," I clarified.

The corners of his lips twitched. "I see that." He pointed to his chest, and I tried not to follow the movement. "For me?"

I nodded and ran my tongue along my bottom lip as my gaze took in the dusting of hair on his pecs that trailed down along his toned stomach before disappearing under his jeans. He cleared his throat and my gaze shot back to his face.

Focus, Izzy. But the slight smirk on his face made me think he knew he was affecting me. Couldn't he put a freaking shirt on for Christ's sake?

"Yes. For you." I huffed. Who else did he think they were for? "The girls and I made them."

He took the container and smiled. "Thanks, Izzy."

Why did I ever complain about his piss poor attitude? It was so much easier to pretend he was unattractive when he was grumpy. This Logan though, with his smile and shy gratitude, was making it awfully hard to avoid how incredibly sexy he was.

"Uh huh." The words came out more as a breathy sound. I needed to get out of there. I couldn't even think straight. "I have plans, so I need to run."

His lips turned down instantly. He obviously didn't like that idea. But at least he wasn't smiling at me anymore.

"Okay." He lifted the container of cookies. "Thank you for the cookies."

"Yup." I turned and hightailed it to my car, freezing when he called my name and glancing back at him over my shoulder.

"Be careful."

I swallowed. The double meaning behind his words sunk in deeply. I needed to be extra careful with the way my body responded to him. That was more dangerous than anything at the bar. I really liked this job, and the last thing I needed was to mess it up because I was crushing hard on my single-dad boss.

I nodded and climbed into my car before backing down the driveway.

But space didn't help when, an hour later, sitting around a high top table with my friends, I still couldn't stop thinking about Logan shirtless and smiling at me.

"Izzy." Lyla snapped her fingers in front of my face. "What's going on with you?"

I shook my head and looked up. "Sorry, it's been a long day."

"Did you work the nanny thing today?" she asked.

I nodded. "Yeah."

"How's that going?" Nicole smirked. "Any other weirdness?"

Oh God. I did not want to go into any of this with this group. I'd never hear the end of it. Izzy crushing on her new boss would not surprise any of them. Nicole and Lyla would tease me relentlessly, while Mia would lecture me.

They all knew my track record. I pick the absolute worst guys to like. Every time. Usually because they were assholes. Not because they were my boss or one of my brother's teammates.

"I told you." I narrowed my eyes slightly in Nicole's direction. "It's fine." I turned back to Lyla. "How's the EMT classes going?"

"Nope. Spill the tea." Mia raised her glass to her lips before shooting me a smirk.

Lyla bounced slightly on her stool. "Yeah, come on. It's not like you to hold out on us. And EMT classes are boring. I could use a little drama."

I sighed. "There's no drama. Nicole just won't let something I said go." I glared over at my friend and brought my glass of cider to my lips.

She shrugged. "I think you like him."

I choked on the liquid I'd taken a sip of.

Lyla tilted her head, glancing between the two of us. "I feel like I'm lost. You like your new boss?"

Nicole giggled. "Remember her brother's teammate she complained about for weeks? The one who flirted with her at the wedding and then almost immediately gave her the cold shoulder?"

Lyla's eyes widened. "Yeah..."

Damn Nicole. I wanted to strangle her.

"He's the single dad she's nannying for."

"Oh my God, no way." Lyla smirked at me. "And didn't you say he's like really hot?"

I sighed. I could feel the disappointment in Mia's look without seeing it. "Yes. But he's my boss now and he's not inter-ested in me anyway, so I'm trying not to go there."

"Liar." Nicole coughed as she said the single word.

"I'm never telling you anything ever again." I should have called or texted my sister that day. Why did I think Nicole was the best option?

She laughed. "I've heard that one before."

"What does she think you're lying about? I'm lost again." Lyla pouted.

I rolled my eyes and huffed. "I told her I thought he was checking me out that first week I'd started nannying. But I was probably just reading into things." I chuckled. "You know me."

"But Nicole's right, you did tell us he was definitely flirting at the wedding," Lyla reminded me.

I shrugged, trying and failing not to remember. Because of all things I was fairly sure of. The way he leaned forward to talk to me. The way his gaze heated when I said I wasn't there with a date. And I surely didn't imagine his eyes drifting down to the cleavage of my dress.

I shifted uncomfortably on my stool. It had only been two months since that day, and it was still fresh in my mind. The way he made me feel. Like not a single other person was in that damn ballroom but me.

"Maybe he was." I schooled my features and shrugged. This wasn't helping. "But that was a one-time thing."

"Back up." Mia narrowed her eyes. "So was he or was he not checking you out a couple weeks ago?"

"Ugh." I crossed my arms. "I don't know. I thought so, but—"

"I'm with Nicole." Mia slapped the table and leaned back. "It's not like you to be unsure. You were convinced he flirted at the wedding, and spent the next few weeks after that determined to figure out why the one-eighty. So now you really like him and are trying to talk yourself out of it?"

"I hate you all."

"Nah." Nicole bumped my shoulder with hers. "You love us. So how about you start from the beginning and tell us everything? Let us actually help you figure it out."

I looked around at their sincere expressions. "Guys," I whined. "There's nothing to figure out. I can't like my new boss, and nothing can happen even if I do like him."

They had to agree. I couldn't imagine they wouldn't, but they all stared at me like they were waiting for me to go on.

Mia would give it to me straight. "Right?" I directed at her across the table.

She shrugged. "I need all the details first. Dating your boss isn't ideal, but dancing around mutual attraction isn't either."

I glanced around at their expressions laced with anticipation, and finally gave in, starting at the beginning—that first night when he came home. I barely took a breath as I poured out the details of the past two weeks, ending with my ridiculous reaction to him when I dropped off the girls and the cookies.

Lyla tapped both hands on the table excitedly. "He's totally into you."

Nicole smirked. "I agree." She tipped her head in my direction. "And she knows it too."

I opened my mouth to respond, but Mia spoke first. I wished I had their confidence.

"But the question is, what's holding him back? Between the way he acted at the wedding and now, he's very hot and cold. Do we want our friend to be with someone like that?"

"Well, maybe it's the same reason she has." Lyla waved in my direction. "About her working for him now."

Mia's brows pulled together suspiciously. "That doesn't account for his behavior at the wedding, or since then. Maybe he's not over his ex-wife."

Before I could respond to that, Nicole was already shaking her head. "I don't think that's it. I've seen them together at the hospital. They seem friendly, but nothing that makes me think anything more. I saw Logan talking to the guy Maggie is dating. They were hitting it off."

Mia's lips turned up into what could only be described as an evil smile. "Text him."

"What?" The words immediately spilled out of my mouth. Was she crazy?

"Yeah. Tell him you've been drinking and need a ride. If he likes you, he won't ask a single question, and he'll come and get you."

I loved Mia, but sometimes I thought something was seriously wrong with her. "I'm not lying to him."

Mia waved me off. "Technically, it's not lying. You have been drinking."

"No." I shook my head. "I'm not doing that. He has the girls, so even if he wanted to, he couldn't."

"That's a good point." Nicole hummed. "But Mia might be onto something. Next time you have a problem, call him first. If he jumps at the chance to help you without question, you have your answer."

"Or that means he's a good person," I countered.

"Eh," Lyla started. "I'm a good person, but even I'm asking questions if you call me for help."

"You guys are ridiculous." But I couldn't help but wonder what he would do if I called and needed help. "Alright, enough of my problems. Lyla, how are the EMT classes going?"

Luckily, they were all willing to finally change the subject. We got a round of shots and toasted Nicole, the birthday girl.

It was one more reminder that I was the baby of the group, only being brought in early this year when I started job sharing with Nicole. Mia was the oldest at twenty-eight, Lyla was a year younger than her, and Nicole was now twenty-five. Maybe that was why they took such an interest in the thing with Logan. They just wanted to make sure I was okay. It felt good, and it was nice that they treated me like a peer and not a little sister.

Our conversation about calling Logan for help aside, I was not one to believe in fate or anything, but as I drove home an hour later and found myself on the side of the road with a flat tire, I had to wonder. I'd only had one cider and one shot, so I was fine to drive. But now I was stuck on the side of a dark road late at night.

My brother had shown me once years ago how to change a tire, but I wasn't confident I remembered, nor did I want to try it in the dark. I picked up my phone and stared at the screen, debating who to call. Jay was the sensible option. I always called him for help.

But the girl's advice ran through my head like a broken record, and before I could chicken out, I dialed Logan's number.

I was about to hang up when his deep voice came through the line. "Izzy? You okay?"

This was dumb. Freaking stupid. How would I explain calling him? He would immediately ask if I had called my brother, and I totally wasn't thinking about the girls. He wasn't going to wake them up and put them in the car to come help me.

"Izzy?"

Shit. "Um. Yeah. Sorry. I..."

"What's wrong? Do you need a ride?" Shuffling noises came through the phone.

My heart took off at a sprint. Was he actually going to come with no questions asked?

"Izzy." This time his voice held a hint of that growliness I'd gotten from him before.

"No. Not a ride. But do you know how to change a tire?"

He scoffed. "Yes, of course. You have a flat?" More rustling came through the line. "Where are you?"

A smirk lifted my lips, and excitement coursed through me. "Just left town, maybe a mile past The Dock."

I held my breath as nerves bubbled up, waiting for his response.

"Okay." He almost seemed distracted.

My body sagged with disappointment when he didn't add anything else. What did I expect? I should have known better than to listen to my friends. They gave the worst advice.

"Dylan's coming over to keep an ear out. I'll be there in a few. Hang tight."

"Oo-okay," I stumbled over the word. "You sure?"

"Yeah. Stay in the car until I get there. Okay?"

"Okay." The call ended and I brought the phone to my chest as a smile lifted my lips. Part of me was afraid to hope this meant more than him just being a good person.

But right now, the excitement that bloomed in my chest was louder than the doubt.

LOGAN

I pulled my truck to a stop behind Izzy's car on the side of the road, grateful to see both her and her car intact. I almost had a heart attack seeing her name pop up on my phone at almost midnight. So many worst-case scenarios had raced through my mind.

She stepped out of her car as I approached, and I fought the groan that bubbled up. What the fuck was she wearing? Did the tight black skirt even cover her whole ass?

"Pop the trunk," I gritted out.

Her brows shot up, and I cursed the way my words were clipped. She turned, bending slightly into the car, and the trunk opened. At least the skirt did in fact cover her ass. But just barely. The shirt, however, looked more like a bra—a strip of fabric across her back, and didn't cover any of her stomach.

I got to work getting the tools and spare out of the back, bringing them around to the driver's side rear tire. I stared at her as she crossed her arms under her chest, pushing her tits up. The pieces of triangle-shaped fabric of her shirt stretched like they struggled to contain her breasts.

I clenched my jaw and squatted down in front of the flat tire. But my brain short-circuited, and I stared at the wheel in front of me as I struggled to remember what I needed to do.

"Are you mad?" she asked.

I wasn't mad. At least not at her. Myself maybe. "No." I shook my head and used the wrench to start breaking the lug nuts.

"Okay..." She shifted on her heels.

I lost the battle not to look at her, my gaze trailing slowly from her black heels up her long legs. Lots of creamy skin that never seemed to end, until finally the black mini skirt came into view. If it wasn't so dark out, I was sure I'd get a glimpse of her panties from this angle. Wonder what color she was wearing? Were they lace? A thong maybe?

"You sure?"

I blinked and pulled my gaze away from her. "Yup." I wasn't sure of anything at the moment, but I answered the question I knew she was asking.

I shoved the jack under the frame of the car and lifted it. *Don't look up*, I reminded myself as I sensed her lean back against the car with a huff. Grabbing the wrench, I continued removing the lug nuts.

"I'm sorry I made you come out," she said, followed by a long sigh. "I probably should have called Jay."

"No." I whipped my gaze up to look at her and the wrench slipped from my hand before clattering to the ground. Dammit. "It's fine." I leaned forward quickly to grab the wrench, and my head collided with the rim. Jesus fucking Christ. I took a calming breath. "I just... need to focus."

"Okay, sorry. You seemed upset."

"I'm not upset." Although now my head hurt, and I felt like I was losing my mind.

I stole another glance up at her as she crossed her arms tighter across her chest with a huff.

"Okay. Whatever."

I stood and crowded her space. The urge to kiss her, to push her up against the car and devour her mouth, was so fucking overwhelming it was torture. Strawberries invaded my senses as I breathed her in. All of it pulled me in deeper. Her jade-colored eyes were wide as she stared back at me. I took another step and braced my hands on either side of her on the car

"Izzy." Her name was barely a whisper on my lips.

"Yes?" Her breath came faster.

Good. I liked that. I wanted so badly to watch her react to my touch, but I kept my hands planted against the car.

"I'm not mad." I zeroed in on her mouth. "However, I'm struggling to focus on changing your tire."

"Oh?"

I tracked the movement of her tongue as it ran along her bottom lip. "Do you know why?"

She shook her head. I didn't believe that. She had to know by now how badly she affected me. But if she needed to hear it, I could at least give her that.

"Because you look so fucking sexy tonight it's killing me." I let my gaze roam down her body, taking my time drinking her in. "Your tits look like they're going to pop out at any minute, and this tiny-ass skirt is giving me so many dirty thoughts."

I groaned before bringing my eyes back to her face. Her mouth hung open. Did that really surprise her? Or was she surprised I admitted it.

"And now I'm thinking about all the men who watched you tonight, who came over and offered to buy you a drink. So am I mad you called me? Fuck no. Because at least that means you didn't go home with any of them."

Was I being possessive over a woman I was sure I wasn't allowed to have? Yes. At that moment did I give a fuck? Nope.

I stared at her lips, that damn gloss glistening, wanting to claim her mouth. Feel her writhe from my touch. But there was a long list of reasons why I couldn't.

I pushed off the car. "Now, would you mind waiting in the car while I change your tire?"

She frowned and crossed her arms over her chest again. Why did I find her pouting over the fact that I didn't kiss her so adorable? I was trying my best to maneuver through this mine-field I'd created.

I reached out and ran my hands down her upper arms. "Please?"

She shivered from my touch and I fucking loved it. Loved that it was obvious I affected her just as much as she did me.

She nodded. "Fine."

I stepped back and she climbed into the car while I got to work changing her tire. This time I had no issues getting the task completed. I put the tools and flat tire in the trunk, closed it, and when I tapped on her window, she opened her car door.

"All good. See you in the morning." I turned and headed to my truck. If she got out and I stayed there any longer, I wouldn't be able to keep my hands to myself this time.

"Wait."

I turned back toward her. She stood outside her car now, arms folded, with a glare trained on me.

"Izzy. Go home, sweetheart." I made my feet stay planted safely five feet away from her. "Before I make a decision neither of us can come back from."

I climbed into my truck and breathed a sigh of relief when she got into her car and drove away. Tomorrow would be rough, that was for sure. But if I was honest, explained the reasons why nothing could happen between us, she would understand.

Wouldn't she?

Chapter Seventeen

LOGAN

My KIDS WERE NEVER early risers, but of course the one morning I needed them to sleep as long as possible, they were up with the sun. I wanted five minutes to talk to Izzy before I dragged them out of bed. But when Izzy walked into the kitchen, I got the feeling it didn't matter. She wasn't outright angry toward me, but she avoided meeting my gaze.

Nikki and Alice were already on their stools on the other side of the island eating bowls of cereal. I half expected them to give me a hard time about not making pancakes. Maybe I'd do that next time I had a morning off with them.

Once the girls finished, they ran into the great room and turned a show on. I glanced at my watch. I only had ten more minutes before I had to leave.

Izzy grabbed the bowls and brought them to the sink. The silence was killing me.

"I wanted to talk about last night." The words tumbled from my mouth quickly.

"What's there to talk about?"

So she wanted to ignore what I said? Act like it didn't happen? Like I didn't almost kiss her?

I should be thankful, but I wasn't.

"Izzy, I—"

"No." Her one-word response held no anger, but it held a lot of surety. She shook her head and turned to me, fists slamming onto her hips. Her voice was barely above a whisper as she spoke. "It's fine. You've been hot and cold since Jay's wedding and obviously have some hang-up. I was stupid last night thinking you coming to change my tire meant anything was different." She took a breath and glanced quickly over to the girls before continuing. "I need this job. I like this job. And I don't need to be let down gently. We're on the same page now, don't worry."

I stared after her as she turned and walked into the great room. Were we on the same page? This was what I wanted, right? To explain to her all the reasons why we couldn't be together. I should be happy. But what I felt was anything but happiness.

And that feeling only intensified as the day went on. Of course, today of all days needed to be a slow day. Only two calls, and both were quick, which left me with a ton of time to harp on what Izzy had said this morning. I tried to busy myself with stupid crap like washing the truck and grabbing a few of the guys to do some drills. But it didn't help keep my mind focused. It kept drifting back to the gorgeous blonde who smelled of strawberries.

What the fuck was wrong with me? I didn't know what I'd expected from her, or what I wanted. And what did she mean when she said she was stupid for thinking me coming to change her tire meant things were different? Did she think I'd tell her no? If I had to, I would have woken the girls and put them in the car.

Her calling her brother never even crossed my mind until she said it.

But now I couldn't stop wondering about it. Why did she call me instead of her brother? Did calling me feel right? Because that was how it felt for me.

My phone vibrating on the table in front of me interrupted my thoughts. I picked it up and clicked on the Google Nest notification, bolting up straight as it alerted me that there was smoke in my kitchen. I glanced at the time. It was after four o'clock, which meant Izzy and the girls should be home by now.

My stomach dropped as I tried calling Izzy and she didn't pick up. What the fuck was going on?

I stood and turned to the guys in the room. "We need to swing by my house." I walked past them. "I'll explain in the truck."

I heard Jay tell Zack to stay behind with the probie. They would be able to grab one of the utility trucks and meet us there if a call came through.

On the way to my house, I updated Jay and Adam, all of us breathing a sigh of relief when we pulled up out front and there was no sign of a fire. But the nerves were back when we walked in the side door and the obvious smell of char hit my nose.

"Izzy?"

She stepped from the great room with her hands on her hips. "Why the heck do you have smoke detectors that talk to you? And how do you shut them up? Because waving a dish towel at it didn't work. She's very passive-aggressive by the way. Repeatedly giving me a heads up that there is smoke in the kitchen. Like really-ly?" She rolled her green eyes. "I couldn't tell."

I chuckled, thankful that everything was okay, and stepped forward. Reaching out, I gripped her shoulder, ready to pull her in for a hug, but froze when her brows rose and she glanced behind me.

I locked my jaw and patted her shoulder. "Glad everything's okay." I let my hand fall back to my side. "What happened?"

In my periphery, I caught Jay's stare, but he wasn't my priority. Izzy was. Although she wore a smile, I could tell she was flustered.

She took a breath before words tumbled from her mouth. "I had cookies in the oven and then Alice came running in and said Nikki fell off the swing set, so I went out back to check on her and she was crying." She took a long pull of air before going on. "Her knee was bleeding and I completely forgot about the cookies. By the time we came back in, the stupid thing was warning me there was smoke in the kitchen. Which again is the dumbest thing I've ever heard. I couldn't get it to shut up. Finally, I opened a bunch of windows and it eventually stopped a few minutes ago."

I nodded. "Sorry about that. I'll have you download the app and sign in so you can turn it off from your phone."

"Or you could be normal and have the cheap battery-operated ones."

A smirk tugged at my lips as I took in her flushed cheeks. "Sorry sweetheart, that's not happening."

Her eyes widened as she stared at me. Fuck. Why did that endearment roll off my tongue so easily now? I could feel Jay's glare burning into me.

"Assuming Nikki's alright now?" I'd deal with Jay if I needed to, once I made sure my family was okay.

She nodded, looking away. "Yes. Just a cut."

"Want me to check it out?" Adam asked, stepping between Jay and me.

I nodded. "Yeah. Thanks."

After making sure everyone was good, we headed back out to the truck. I climbed into the driver's seat as usual and let out a sigh when Jay climbed up into the passenger seat. Awesome.

The door wasn't even shut all the way before he turned to me with a glare. "You two sleeping together?"

I shook my head. "No." At least that I could answer without lying.

"This should be fun," Adam mumbled.

Jay sent him a glare before turning back to me. "That's either a lie or a not yet."

I swallowed, but kept quiet.

"So which one is it?" Jay scoffed. "My bet is on the latter because I don't think you'd outright lie to me." He rubbed a hand down his face. "She's too young for you," he spat out.

"I agree." That part I could comment on. But I didn't understand why I couldn't utter the words I knew he wanted me to.

"And she really needs that job. Don't mess that up for her."

I nodded. "Not planning on it."

"Damn it, man. I mean it." The glare was back.

I stopped at a red light and turned to look at him. "I hear you, loud and clear."

He didn't want me dating his sister, and I got it. I hadn't expected anything else.

The rest of the shift felt like forever. I wanted to get out of there. Jay didn't say another word to me, and barely even looked at me.

Adam stepped up next to me at the counter as I finished washing the dishes from dinner. "Can I give you some advice?"

"I don't need advice."

He sighed. "Well, pretend you do. Pretend there's a chance something might happen with Izzy."

I narrowed my eyes on him. "There's not."

He cocked a brow and waited.

Who was I kidding? All I could think about all day was pulling Izzy into my arms. How I was as worried about her as I was about my kids. Even I wasn't sure I could keep resisting the pull between us.

I thrust a plate at him. "If you're going to give out unsolicited advice, at least help dry."

He grabbed a dish towel and started drying. "Tell Jay you like her."

"What?" I looked back over at him, trying to figure out how that would help me.

117

"If he knows you want something serious with her, he'll be more on board."

I handed him another plate. "I want advice on how not to go there, not how to make Jay okay with it, dumbass."

He chuckled. "From what I saw today, I think we're past that. Now it's about making the fallout not as bad."

I huffed and continued to wash the dishes as I thought over what he said. I agreed with Jay. Izzy was too young for me. My life came with baggage that wasn't fair to her. She was barely old enough to drink and go out to bars.

And the one thing I was sure of? If I went there with her, it wouldn't be a one-time thing. She'd be mine.

Chapter Eighteen

IZZY

Lyla: So any update on the sexy single dad situation?

Me: Where do I start?

Me: I got a flat on my way home from the bar last night and ended up calling him...

Nicole: Yay! Did he come without question?

Me: Yup.

Mia: Told you. So there ya go. You got your answer. Now what are you going to do about it?

Me: Not so fast. It's more complicated than that.

Mia: How?

Nicole: Let her fill us in.

Me: He said the absolute sexiest things and then almost kissed me. But after he changed my tire, he told me to go home and walked away from me.

Me: Then I decided I didn't care. I was over his game. So this morning I basically told him that.

Mia: Attagirl!

Me: Yup.

Nicole: But?

Me: Ugh. But then he almost hugged me in front of my brother this afternoon and called me sweetheart.

Me: Like seriously, what do I do?

Mia: Screw him. And I don't mean literally.

Lyla: He called you sweetheart in front of Jay? Sounds to me like you have your answer. Now you need to decide if you like him enough to give him a chance.

Nicole: Have you seen or talked to him since then?

Me: No.

Nicole: I think it all depends on what he says when he gets home tonight.

Lyla: True. Keep us posted!

~

THE LAST THREE hours crawled by. Probably because I was back to second-guessing where I stood with Logan. He made me so mad I could scream. But the minute he gripped my shoulder and went to pull me in for a hug, freaking stupid butterflies took off in my stomach.

And then he called me sweetheart again. In front of my brother. Like what the hell?

I made it super freaking clear this morning that I was done playing this hot and cold game with him. Did I jump to conclusions? Although I didn't think so after the way he walked away last night. Damn him and making me question everything again.

I finished up the girls' bedtime routine and busied myself by cleaning up the kitchen. I held my breath when I heard the front door open and close. Drying my hands, I spun just in time to see him step into the kitchen.

We stood there, staring at each other. I could feel my heart beating in my chest, scared to move or say anything that would ruin whatever moment we were having. Because the way he looked at me—it stole my breath. And just like last night, I wanted more.

My breath hitched as he began moving toward me with a determination I could feel, and I made my feet move, meeting him halfway. His arms wrapped around my back as mine wound around his neck. Pulling me against him, he lifted me slightly off the ground and claimed my mouth.

Holy hell, could he kiss. His tongue demanded access, and he explored every inch of my mouth. My breaths came faster, and my core throbbed. Had I ever felt this turned on? This desperate?

His hands moved down and gripped me tight under my ass, lifting me up higher. I wrapped my legs around his waist, and felt his hard cock press into me. I moaned into his mouth as he backed me against the counter and rotated his hips.

Oh my God. That spurred him on, and he did it again,

balancing me on the edge of the counter. His hands trailed up over my hips and slid beneath my shirt. His warm, rough hands along my skin sent a shiver racing down my spine.

My phone ringing from somewhere nearby penetrated through the lust-induced haze I was in. He slowed the kiss and pulled back. Our breaths came in pants as we stared at each other. There were questions in his eyes that I was sure matched my own.

What were we doing? What did this mean?

My phone began ringing again.

"You should probably get that." His lips lifted into a smirk. "Unless you want to ignore it."

Oh, I really wanted to ignore it. But I was pretty sure it was the third time it had gone off.

"Let me make sure it's nothing important."

He nodded and stepped back, lowering me slowly to my feet.

I grabbed my phone, my brother's name flashing on the screen. I slid the answer button up and brought it to my ear. "What's up?"

"Mom fell down the stairs."

"What?" I blinked. "Is she okay?"

"Dad thinks she broke her hip. They're at the hospital." A door shutting came through the line. "I'm heading there now. Want me to swing by and pick you up?"

My siblings and I didn't grow up in Half Moon Lake. We grew up in a town about thirty minutes away, where my parents still lived. I glanced over at Logan. Did I want to leave right now? No, not really. Part of me really wanted to stay. But it was my mom. She'd been there every single time I needed something, no way I wouldn't be there for her. And since I couldn't get an appointment to get a new tire until tomorrow, I didn't want to drive my car that far.

"Sure. I'm still at Logan's. Can you pick me up here?"

Logan's eyebrows pulled together, and Jay scoffed. Maybe I didn't want to drive with him after all. I knew he was pissed when Logan called me sweetheart earlier. But if he wanted to have that conversation with me, I had no problem telling his ass off. Sometimes he treated me like I was still twelve and he needed to take care of me.

"Or I can drive myself."

"No, I'm on my way. Be there in a few."

"Okay." I ended the call and put my phone down, taking in Logan's concerned expression. "My mom fell down the stairs."

"Shit." Logan closed the space between us and pulled me back into his chest, wrapping his arms tight around my back. "Was that Jay?"

I nodded. "Yeah. He's coming to pick me up."

"I heard." He sighed. "Wish I could drive you."

I smiled, listening to his heart beat, the sentiment of his words meaning just as much as the words themselves. "I know."

I melted into his hold, not wanting our moment to end. But when my phone chimed with a notification, I reluctantly pulled away and gathered my stuff.

"I'll see you tomorrow morning." I took a step toward him and reached up. Using my thumb, I wiped my lip gloss from under his bottom lip.

He caught my hand and pressed his lips to the inside of my palm. And damn, the butterflies were back.

"Text me when you get home tonight."

I started to shake my head, but he gripped my chin with his finger and thumb.

"Need to know you got home safe and how your mom's doing."

When I nodded, he leaned forward and brushed his lips gently against mine. My phone chimed again.

I pulled away with a roll of my eyes. "I'd better go."

He followed me and stood in the doorway as I made my way down the sidewalk to Jay's car. I sent him a wave and a smile before sliding into the passenger seat.

I waited patiently for my brother's lecture. Or disapproval. Or both.

"Please tell me nothing's going on between you and Logan."

I sighed and tried not to sound like a petulant child. "That's not really any of your business." He knew my track record for shitty boyfriends, and had given me plenty of lectures. Logan was the complete opposite. A good guy. So I couldn't help but wonder what his issue was.

"He's too old for you."

Ah, here we go. He was leading with that? Really?

"Seriously?" I chuckled. "Um, couldn't I say the same for you and Sarah? She's what, like eight years older than you?"

He glanced over with raised eyebrows. "That's not the same."

"How so?" I crossed my arms over my chest. "Because I'm a girl?" Double standard much?

"No. I—" He shook his head. "Because you're only twenty-one."

"Okay, and you were twenty-five when you met Sarah."

"He's divorced and has two kids."

I rolled my eyes. "And Sarah was a single mom with a baby."

The silence grew in the car until I felt tears form behind my eyes. Of all the people in my life, I wanted my big brother to be proud of me. He'd always taken care of me, sacrificed so much to do so, and now I was trying to take care of myself. To show him I could do it.

I wanted him to finally look at me as mature and grown-up. But the last couple of years, that felt more and more unattainable. Like, no matter what I did, he would only ever see me as his impulsive twelve-year-old little sister.

"You know, you could just be happy for me." I sniffed.

"Jesus," he mumbled. "Izzy, I'm trying to look out for you." A deep sigh escaped him. "Do you really think getting tied down with a family right now is what's best for you?"

I whipped my gaze over to him. "I'm not entirely sure what's best for me right now. But what I do know is it's up to me to figure that out, don't you think?" I huffed and sagged back into

124

the seat. "What would you have said to me if I said this to you when you started things with Sarah?"

He glanced over, studying me. "I would have told you to shut it."

"Right."

He was silent for the next several minutes, and I could practically feel him processing his reaction. "You really like him?"

My lips lifted into a smile. "I do." I chuckled. "Can I tell you a story?"

He knew better than anyone that my exes were self-centered pricks who would do nothing for me that didn't benefit themselves. So when he nodded, I gave him the SparkNotes version of what happened the night before. Getting the flat and calling Logan. Him coming to help me without a single question. I left off the things he said to me about how I affected him. I doubted my brother wanted those details.

"Hmm," he said, a smirk tugging at his lips. "He didn't even ask if you called me first?"

I shook my head. "Nope. And when I said maybe I should have, he acted like the idea offended him. Like, why would I call anyone but him?"

He was quiet again for far too long before finally speaking again. "You could lose the nanny gig if it doesn't work out."

That thought sent my stomach plummeting. But I was aware that was a risk. "Isn't there some famous quote that says the greatest failure is not to try?"

With a chuckle, he shook his head, and after a moment, he said, "You know I'll kick his ass if he breaks your heart."

"Jay," I began, searching for the right words. I appreciated the sentiment, but I needed him to understand something. "I'm not your baby sister who needs protecting anymore."

He scoffed, and I rolled my eyes. Maybe that was asking too much from him tonight. To him, I might always be the baby sister who needs him.

Chapter Nineteen

LOGAN

My phone chiming loudly stirred me from sleep, and I grabbed it from my nightstand. Was it really past midnight? I clicked on the text notification from Izzy.

Izzy: Home now. You awake?

> Me: Yeah. Thought maybe I'd hear you when Jay dropped you back off at your car.

Izzy: He didn't. I was exhausted so he brought me back to the apartment. He said he'll drop me off at your place on his way in tomorrow.

> Me: Oh. How's your mom?

Izzy: In pain. Hip definitely broken. She's going to need PT.

Me: Sorry to hear.

Me: Did Maggie tell you the plan for tomorrow night?

Izzy: Yeah. The donuts with grown-ups thing. I'll take the girls, she'll meet me there.

Me: Yes. and I'm going to try to swing by if I can.

Tomorrow night was supposed to continue my five-day stretch with the twins, but as I wasn't sure I could make the donut thing work with my schedule, we planned for Maggie to take them and then keep them overnight. Although we'd decided this before hiring Izzy, we agreed to stick to it since it made the most sense. We had a set parenting schedule, but since we got along well, it made making changes and adjustments easy.

Izzy: Ok. Why do they do donuts at 6:30 in the evening?

Me: No idea. I think it used to be in the morning and then everyone complained so now they kept the name and moved it to the evening.

Me: I don't eat the donuts.

Izzy: Of course you don't.

Me: What's that supposed to mean?

Izzy: Pretty sure you don't have all those muscles from eating donuts.

Me: You've been checking out my muscles?

Izzy: Kinda hard not to when you wear those skintight shirts all the time.

Me: Hmm. You like those?

Izzy: Maybe. Shirtless was nice too. ;)

Me: You blushing and flustered was adorable.

Izzy: What? I wasn't flustered. And I didn't blush.

Me: Totally did. But I liked it. The way you looked at me and how cute you were. Even more of a motivation now to get my workouts in. I typically try to stay away from carbs and sugars. But then you made me really delicious cookies and I ate the entire container.

Izzy: The girls made you cookies.

Me: Hmm. They tell a slightly different story.

Izzy: Traitors. All I did was ask if they wanted to make some for their dad too.

Izzy: It's late. 6am is going to come quickly. We should probably get to bed.

Me: Yeah...

Izzy: Goodnight, Logan.

Me: Night.

I put my phone down and fell back on the pillow. My eyes drifted closed, and images of her balanced on the edge of the counter last night, lips pink and swollen from my kiss, ran through my mind. I wasn't sure what my next move was, but Adam's advice echoed through my thoughts. I'd crossed that line, and I had no intention of going back. Now, it was all about minimizing the fallout.

Sleep eluded me most of the night. I finally got up at five and headed to the basement to work out, needing to burn off this tension that plagued me. But it didn't do much to help, and when Izzy walked in at six thirty in cutoffs and another crop top, I was right back to feeling like a tightrope.

"Ooh." A smirk pulled at her lips. "Are we back to growly papa bear?"

I stalked toward her, causing her to take a few steps back, and caged her in with my hands braced on the wall. She angled her head back and I locked on her lips, pink and glistening.

"How many crop tops do you own?"

"So many." Her tongue ran along her bottom lip and she reached up, tracing the outline of my pec through my T-shirt. "How many of these insanely tight T-shirts do you own?"

My muscle twitched under her touch. "A lot." I closed my eyes as she trailed her finger up to my shoulder and down over my bicep. Her touch felt so good. I never wanted her to stop.

"Logan." My name was a breathy whisper on her lips.

I opened my eyes and stared at her. Her green eyes had darkened and were focused on my mouth. I knew what she wanted. The same thing I wanted. I removed one hand from the wall and threaded my fingers through her long, silky locks. I leaned down, tightening my hold on her hair and pulling her mouth to meet mine. Our lips brushed. Once, twice, and then... Footsteps sounded on the stairs.

I smiled against her lips before breaking the kiss and untangling my hand from her hair. The girls rounded the bottom of the steps, and I turned to face them as they barreled into the kitchen.

"Slow down, speed racers," I teased. I grabbed my duffle and slung the strap over my head. "Izzy will drive you guys to the donut thing tonight, and Mom will meet you there."

"And you too?" Nikki climbed up on her stool at the counter.

"I am going to try. But no promises." Sometimes I hated that my job didn't allow me to fully commit to things. But at least the girls were good about understanding.

Izzy brushed past me, heading further into the kitchen. "Pancakes again, girls?"

"Yes!" they exclaimed.

My lips lifted into a smile as I took a minute to watch Izzy move around the kitchen. As if she could sense my appraisal, she glanced over at me and tilted her head, her long blonde hair falling down over her shoulder.

I still wasn't sure what I had to offer, but there was no denying I wanted the chance to show her.

Chapter Twenty

IZZY

WEDNESDAY 10:15 A.M.

Me: So I'm going to need more advice.

Mia: ....

Nicole: Oh boy.

Me: He kissed me.

Lyla: GIF of a woman jumping up and down excitedly

Nicole: I'm confused...what advice do you need?

Mia: Don't sleep with him. I'd make him grovel and work for it now.

Me: We haven't really talked... Like about what this means, what we're doing and all that.

Lyla: Give it time. Things are complicated. You're not only his nanny, you're also Jay's sister. Take it slow, one day at a time. And yeah, don't sleep with him until you know he's not just trying to bang the nanny.

Me: 🙂

Nicole: I agree. Don't push him for a label, but also don't take things further until you guys have that talk.

Chapter Twenty-One

IZZY

I WAVED at Maggie as she stepped through the doors of the school's cafeteria. I hadn't rushed to get here, knowing she wouldn't be here until closer to seven. We'd only gotten here ten minutes ago and grabbed seats at a table. Maggie spotted me and made her way toward us.

"Can we get donuts now?" Nikki asked, popping up on her knees.

"Of course." Maggie smiled.

They both jumped up and ran toward the line.

"You coming?" she directed at me.

I shook my head. "I'm good on the donuts." I'd watched at least five kids take a donut only to put it back, and at least two sneeze over a bunch in line. I wasn't a germaphobe, but I also couldn't afford to get sick right now. "I'll wait here and save the seats until you guys get back. "

"Okay. Thanks." She hurried over and stood in line with the girls.

The line moved slowly as they inched closer to the front. I picked up my phone and opened Instagram, scrolling through the feed to pass the time. Excitement coursed through me when a text from Logan appeared in my notifications.

> Logan: Just parked. You guys inside?

> Me: Yes. I'm sitting at a table. Maggie's in line with the girls.

> Logan: Heading in.

I glanced over at Maggie, who was focused on something Alice was telling her. Would it be weird with both of them here? Nicole might've been convinced nothing lingered between them, but I'd only been working at the hospital since January, so I hadn't seen the two of them together in the same space. In fact...I couldn't remember if I'd ever seen them together.

My gaze landed on Logan as he weaved through the mass of tables. He sat down across from me, and the smile he sent me had my stomach fluttering again. His dark hair was wet and he looked so sexy in a Henley, especially with the top three buttons undone.

"Hi," he said, leaning forward and bracing his arms on the table.

"Hey." I tucked my hair behind my ear as his gaze followed my movements.

"How was your day?"

"Good." I tapped my nails on the table but stopped when he zeroed in on the nervous habit. Why was I even nervous? "Worked at the hospital, and the girls and I made meatloaf."

His eyes widened. "Meatloaf?"

"I heard it's your favorite." My lips twitched as I fought a smirk. "Lucky for you, we saved you some."

"Can't wait." He slanted farther toward me and lowered his voice. "Although there's something else I'm craving."

His gaze heated as he kept it trained on me, and I squirmed in my seat. The way he could make me feel like I was the only woman in the room was unlike anything I'd experienced.

"Daddy," Nikki's voice broke through the moment. "You came."

Logan shifted to wrap his arm around his daughter as she clamored up onto the bench next to him. "I couldn't stay away from my favorite girls."

Alice took the spot next to me, and Maggie sat on the other side of Nikki.

"Daddy, you need to get your donut before they're all gone."

Logan nodded and stood. "What kind do you want, Izzy?"

"I'm good." I kept my gaze averted, suddenly feeling like I was intruding on their time together as a family. "I probably should get going."

"No, stay," Logan and Maggie said in unison.

My gaze shot to Maggie, who smirked at Logan before focusing on me. "The girls want you here, you should stay."

"Please, Izzy?" both girls whined.

I sighed. "Okay."

"So am I surprising you, or do you have a preference?" Logan asked.

I peered up at him, trying not to stare at the outline of muscles under his shirt. "Surprise me."

"Jelly filled it is," he said with a chuckle before walking away.

God, I hoped he was kidding. Who liked jelly-filled?

Both girls had ones with chocolate icing and sprinkles. Maggie looked like she had some type of cruller. I was curious to see what Logan would come back with.

Thankfully, Alice and Nikki filled the time chatting nonstop about school and how excited they were for soccer practice.

"Can we go make the craft?" Alice pointed to the tables on the other side of the cafeteria where they were making paper plate donuts.

Maggie nodded. "Sure."

The girls ran off and I tapped my fingers on the table, hoping Logan made it back quickly. The way Maggie was staring at me reminded me a lot of the look my mom would give me whenever she knew I had done something and needed to confess. But there was no way I planned on telling her I kissed her ex-husband.

"Ugh, that woman needs to get a clue." Maggie's eyes narrowed in the direction where Logan was standing, two donuts in hand, talking to the same woman who was at soccer practice.

The reminder that they had talked about getting together for coffee sent my stomach plummeting.

"A clue?" I focused back on Maggie. I couldn't watch the woman flirt with Logan while he smiled at her.

"Yeah, she's relentless. Hasn't caught on that Logan isn't interested." Maggie huffed.

"How do you know?" I peered back over, taking in the way he smiled and nodded as she talked. He did agree to get coffee with her last week when she approached him at the soccer field. I turned back to Maggie.

She shrugged. "She's been flirting with him since the beginning of the school year. If he was interested at all, he would have already asked her out."

"They did agree to meet for coffee." The words spilled from my lips before I truly thought about them.

Her eyes widened a tad, but she shook her head. "I'll believe it when I see it. Trust me, he does not like that woman."

I shifted uncomfortably. She said it like she was trying to convince me. Could she sense there was something going on? How would she feel about that if she knew?

"Look, Logan's a good guy. I want him to find someone he can build a relationship with, but it's definitely not her. And he's too nice to tell her he's not into her." She stared at me for a moment too long before a smirk pulled at her lips. "I think once he finally finds the perfect someone, he'll be all in."

I swallowed. The way she kept studying me as she talked made me squirm.

"Christ," Logan said, startling me as he appeared at the table and slid into his seat. "Never thought I'd get away this time. She's relentless."

Maggie's lips lifted into a smirk as she mouthed *told you*. "You need to tell her she's barking up the wrong tree."

He kept his gaze trained on me for a beat before glancing over at Maggie. "I told her she needs to talk to Zack about fire safety week. That he handles all that, and I have no idea of the schedule."

"Smart." She chuckled. "Zack will have no problem shamelessly flirting with her."

He focused back on me. "That's my hope. Then maybe she'll leave me alone."

Nikki and Alice appeared, cutting our conversation short and waving the colorful donut crafts in their hands, excitedly showing them to all of us.

"I'd better get them home. It's almost past their bedtime." Maggie pushed to her feet. "Thanks for bringing them tonight, Izzy. That was such a huge help."

I nodded. "No problem."

Once everyone said their goodbyes, Maggie and the girls headed for the exit. Logan stood, that intense stare of his burning into me as I rose to my feet. I swallowed, almost nervously, because I could clearly see the need radiating off him.

"I'll walk you out." The majority of kids and parents had already emptied out, and his hand landed on my lower back as he ushered me in front of him toward the double doors that led out of the cafeteria.

Once outside in the parking lot, I slowed my feet and pointed toward my car a few rows over. I'd brought my car because I'd planned to leave from here to head home. "I'm over this way."

He nodded and gestured up the row in front of us. "Okay. I'm up here. I'll drive you over."

I tilted my head. My car was literally fifty feet away. But the way he was looking at me sent excitement racing down my spine, and I nodded. Anticipation bubbled up as we walked to his truck. The minute I had my door closed, he was backing his truck up and heading to the other side of the lot, passing the row my car was parked in without a second glance. I couldn't help but smile.

He pulled into an empty spot, throwing it into park and turning toward me. "I feel like a teenager again." His fingers threaded through my hair, and he pulled me toward him. "But I need to kiss you."

Our mouths fused, and my core tightened as his tongue pushed its way past my lips. I leaned further over the console trying to get closer to him, needing to be closer. As if he could sense my need, he broke the kiss and reached down, lifting the lever that pushed his seat back. I clamored over the console as he gripped my hips and guided me to straddle him.

"Fuck, these shorts." His fingers dug into the bottom of my asscheeks, now exposed since my cutoffs had risen up.

I pressed my palms against his chest, pushing him back against the seat, and moved my hips forward, grinding against him, loving the groan that slipped from his lips as he threw his head back. I did it again, watching his face as he fought against the pleasure. After the third time, his fingers dug into my hips, preventing me from doing it again.

"Sweetheart," he hissed out between clenched teeth. His gaze softened as he stared at me, bringing his hands up to cup my face. "I've thought about this all day. About kissing you again. I could barely think about anything else."

I smiled, and those ridiculous butterflies took off in my stomach again. I leaned forward, pressing my lips to his. What started off as slow and gentle quickly turned into desperate and passionate. It was such a new thing for me. I was so turned on I couldn't stop my hips from moving again, seeking friction.

I moaned into his mouth, and after a moment, I pulled back. Was I really trying to get off by rubbing myself shamelessly against him?

He stared at me and tucked my hair behind my ear. "There's so much we need to talk about."

I nodded and focused my gaze on his chest, suddenly feeling nervous. "I know."

He gripped my chin, tipping my head up so I met his intense gaze. "I like you, Izzy. Far more than I should. You're young, and I'm not sure what I have to offer you."

I opened my mouth to respond because I wasn't sure what he meant, but he quickly went on.

"My life revolves around my girls and my job. You could find a young guy who could give you the things I can't right now. But selfishly, I want you to myself."

"I don't want anyone else." I shook my head. I didn't want to come off desperate, but I needed him to understand. "I like you too. And I get your life is busy and you have a lot of responsibilities." I blew out a breath, trying to find the words to ease his worry. But maybe the answer was simpler. "Can't we just see where this goes?"

He stiffened but quickly relaxed, and I wasn't sure if I'd said the right thing or not. It was hard. On one hand, I understood the restrictions we would face. But when I really thought of those restrictions, they didn't bother me. Maybe allowing time to show him that would be best.

"Yeah." He searched my face before pulling my head forward and pressing his lips to my forehead. "We can do that."

But his tone made it seem like that wasn't what he wanted.

LOGAN

I couldn't blame her for not wanting to label this quite yet. But the need to make her mine still coursed through me as we got out of my truck and walked the few feet back to her car.

"I start night shifts tomorrow for three days." Tonight was supposed to be my first shift of a four-night rotation, but I switched with someone so I could try to make it to donuts with grown-ups. Either way would have been a crap shoot, but I thought there would be more of a chance if I had the day shift. That was also why Maggie and I came up with a backup plan in case I got stuck on shift.

She nodded, leaning back against her car. "Yeah, I saw that on the schedule. And I go to Maggie's tomorrow morning?"

"Yeah, sorry for the chaotic change."

"Nah, it's fine. I get you guys planned this before hiring me."

Disappointment landed in my gut at the realization that I wouldn't see her until tomorrow night, and it would only be for a few minutes before I'd have to leave for my shift. "Can I come by and take you to lunch tomorrow?"

She smiled and nodded. "I work at the hospital. My lunch break is at noon."

I reached out and tucked her hair behind her ear, letting my fingers trail down the side of her neck. My lips lifted into a smirk as she shivered from the barely there touch.

"I can't wait to try the meatloaf." I continued my path down her body, skimming over the side of her breast and the bare skin below where her crop top ended. "I bet it's delicious."

Her breath hitched and I took another step forward. With a finger under her chin, I lifted her face as I leaned down and claimed her mouth, pulling her hard against my body with my other hand anchored to her waist.

It was dark now, and there were only a few cars left in the lot, but the last thing I wanted was for Izzy to be the subject of small-town gossip. Thankfully, the dark-tinted windows on my truck allowed us privacy, but standing out here by her car could be a problem.

Reluctantly, I pulled back and pressed my lips to her forehead. "Text me when you get home."

"Okay."

Her breaths came in small pants, and her cheeks still held a twinge of pink. I fucking loved it. I opened her car door, letting her climb in before shutting the door and stepping back. I stood there until she pulled out onto the main road.

The entire drive home, I replayed the way she looked straddling my lap as she moved against me—the way her cheeks flushed and her lips were red and swollen from my kiss.

The house was quiet. Too quiet. I wanted to invite Izzy back here. But I knew what that would lead to, and I didn't want to go there until I was sure. Or rather, until she was sure. Because yeah, I had my doubts, but they weren't about what I wanted. I'd been fighting this for almost six months, and now that I'd bulldozed through all the walls I'd put up, I didn't plan on changing my mind.

But Izzy might. Once she saw the limited amount of time I had outside of my job and the girls, she might decide I wasn't worth it. That thought sat heavy and uncomfortable in my gut.

I warmed up the meatloaf, and when my phone vibrated in my pocket, I pulled it out, pulling up the text thread with Izzy.

Izzy: I'm home.

Me: Good. I'm about to try your meatloaf.

I set my phone down and took the plate from the microwave before grabbing a fork. I looked down at the phone again when it vibrated on the counter.

Izzy: There's a small container of sauce in the fridge too. Make sure to put that on it.

After getting out the sauce and warming it, I spread it over the meatloaf and took a bite. Damn. My eyes rolled back in my head as I savored the taste. I picked up my phone and typed out another text.

Me: This is really good. Do you use a recipe? I like to save ones that both the girls and I like.

Izzy: Um, kinda. If I try something new I'll use a recipe, but after that I go off memory. But hold on, I think I can find the one I used for this years ago.

Izzy: *link to meatloaf recipe*

Me: Thanks.

I finished the food and washed the plate before grabbing my phone and heading into the great room. After turning the TV on, I relaxed back on the couch and typed out another message.

Me: What are you up to?

Izzy: Watching TV. You?

Me: Same.

Although the baseball game was playing and I was only half paying attention.

Me: What are you watching?

Izzy: The Night Agent.

I chuckled.

Me: Really?

Izzy: Why does that surprise you? Because I'm a girl?

Me: Not surprising. It's one of my favorite shows too.

Izzy: Oh.

Me: Yeah. But I read the book first.

Izzy: I binged the first season last year and then went and read the book.

Izzy: I'm also obsessed with Yellowjackets. Have you watched that one?

Me: No. Is that the one about people surviving in the wilderness after a plane crash?

Izzy: Yes! It's a high school girls soccer team. Kinda dark. But so good.

We texted back and forth about the shows we watched, and it became obvious she really liked the darker thrillers. That was actually surprising, considering she was so carefree—the complete opposite of dark.

She hadn't responded to my last two texts by the time I went upstairs and turned on the shower. Was she the type of person who fell asleep easily? That thought led to dirty ones of her in my bed. Naked and writhing under me as I drilled into her over and over again.

I always showered quickly after a shift, but tonight I needed another nice long, cold one. I stepped under the water and braced one hand against the wall as I fisted my hard cock with my other hand. I moved my hand roughly up and down my shaft as I pictured Izzy spread out on my bed, and then above me, riding my cock. Mouth open, cheeks flushed, and head thrown back— just like she was tonight—as she moved. But in my mind, I imagined nothing between us as she chased her orgasm.

"Fuck," I bellowed as I exploded, imagining what she'd look like as she came with me.

The need to be with her still overwhelmed me as I climbed into bed and shot off one last text.

> Me: Goodnight, sweetheart.

Chapter Twenty-Two

IZZY

"LOGAN WILL PICK the kids up from school and take them to soccer this afternoon." Maggie moved around her kitchen as she made her to-go cup of coffee. "I'm not sure I'll make it. You'll need to be at Logan's by six thirty."

Logan would have the girls back until Sunday afternoon. Honestly, I had no clue how either of them could stand to be away from them that long. It definitely helped that they got along and made sure they were both there for their daughters when possible, regardless of whose day it was.

I nodded. "Sounds good."

Tonight would be my first night shift at Logan's. I was basically getting paid to spend the night at his house. I just wished he would be there with me.

Maggie looked over at me like she either knew where my thoughts went or wanted to say something else, but uncertainty flashed through her eyes before she finally turned away. The girls appeared, giving her hugs goodbye, and before the door even closed behind her, they were already getting out the tools and ingredients for breakfast.

"Can we make French toast?" Alice asked as she pulled the loaf of bread from the bread box on the counter.

"Of course." One of the things I enjoyed most was baking and cooking with them, especially since, between the two of them, they were willing to try just about anything. So far, I'd learned that neither of them liked beans, Alice didn't like bananas, and Nikki wasn't a fan of cheese. I grabbed my phone and brought up my music app. "What do you want to listen to?"

"Taylor Swift," Nikki said as Alice nodded her agreement.

Not sure why I even asked. That was always their response. I got the music started, and we prepared the egg mixture for the French toast. They laughed at me when I used the whisk to lip sync along to Taylor's voice.

"You're so funny." Alice giggled.

We finished up, and once they were at the small table of the eat-in kitchen, I cleaned up the mess we made.

"Alright, girlies." I grabbed their plates. "Run and get dressed and brush your teeth."

They darted out of the room and I shook my head, chuckling. I didn't literally mean run. My phone chimed and I pulled it out of my back pocket. A smile tugged at my lips as I clicked on the text notification from Logan.

> Logan: Did you want to swing by and grab the SUV?

Did I care if I used the SUV today instead of my car? Not particularly. But even though I was seeing him for lunch today, the thought of seeing him for a minute this morning excited me.

> Me: Sure. I'll swing by.

I had to kind of pass his house to get to the elementary school anyway, so why not?

> Logan: You can use it to go to and from the hospital too, so you can go straight from dropping them off and it'll save you on gas.
>
> Me: Are you sure?

That would actually be easier.

> Logan: Yes. I'm going to give you the spare key so you have it. Feel free to use it anytime you need it.

> Me: Ok. Thanks.

Did he just offer me the use of his car whenever I needed it? He probably meant anytime I needed to use it for driving his kids around.

After packing their lunches, I threw them in their backpacks before ushering them out the door and heading toward Logan's house. I parked my car on the street, and the girls climbed out onto the sidewalk as I walked around the front of my car. Logan opened the front door and made his way down the sidewalk.

"Daddy," both girls squealed, taking off toward their father.

I smiled as he lifted each of them up with one arm. Every time he did that it amazed me, reminding me how strong and muscular he was. As he got closer, I read his shirt and laughed. *Firefighter Dad: Like a normal dad, but badass.*

"Cute shirt," I said as he came to a stop in front of me.

"Thanks." He looked between his daughters. "The girls got it for me for Christmas."

The smile he aimed at me had my stomach fluttering, and the way he held my gaze so intently reminded me of two months ago at Jay's wedding. I was so sure then that something lay between us, and now I didn't have to question that anymore.

"Alright, girls." He kissed the tops of their heads. "In the car. Izzy needs to get you two to school." He sat them down and they ran to the SUV parked in the driveway.

He took a step toward me and then another, his gaze trained on my face, and held the key to the SUV out toward me. "Here."

Our fingers brushed as I took the key from him, both of us lingering at the touch.

"Use it anytime you need to." He glanced over his shoulder toward the SUV before looking back at me. "And I ordered you a credit card you can use for gas and such."

"Thank you." I shifted, trying to tamp down the way my stomach flipped from his touch. "I'd better get going."

His hand twitched like he wanted to reach out. But I understood not wanting the girls to ask questions that neither of us had the answers to quite yet. I brushed past him and smiled as he reached out with one finger to trail along the back of my hand.

Alice and Nikki chatted excitedly in the back seat during the short drive to school, and all I could think about was their father. He was everything I'd ever hoped for and more. And I was intent on showing him exactly that.

Chapter Twenty-Three

LOGAN

I STOOD on my front lawn until the white SUV turned down the next street toward the elementary school. The need to reach out and pull her toward me was so strong, and yet I knew I couldn't. At least not yet. Not only did I want Izzy to be sure this was what she wanted before telling the girls, but I owed Maggie a conversation before then too. She did the same for me when she started seeing Jesse, and it became serious enough to bring him around our daughters.

I turned to head back inside, but stopped when I saw Dylan heading toward me from his house.

"Hey man," he called, jogging over.

"Hey. What's up?"

"Wanted to give you a heads up on what we found."

I really had no expectations from the matchbook I'd found. It could have been dropped by anyone. And honestly, I didn't expect an update. It wasn't like I was officially involved in the case at all.

"Really?" My tone held an obvious hint of skepticism.

"Well, off the books, of course," he said with a smirk. "But Violet was able to pull prints that tracked back to the owner of the business. We had to turn it over to the fire investigators, but they're letting the department help out."

"That's great. So are they looking at the owner then?"

He shook his head. "No. The guy's dead."

"You for real?"

"Yup. Died from pneumonia almost a year ago. But get this— you all pulled him from a fire almost seven years ago." He tipped his chin slightly toward me. "Violet thinks it's the son. She turned over her findings, and the investigators are supposed to go talk to him today."

"Hmm," I rubbed the side of my face with one hand. "Do you know anything about the fire?" I'd been with the Half Moon Lake FD for the last twelve years, surely I'd remember him if I was the one who pulled him from the fire.

"Outskirts of town, large farmhouse. Son was thirteen, maybe fourteen. Both him and mom were checked at the scene and cleared, but dad had to be rushed to the hospital for smoke inhalation."

"I remember that one." I shook my head. "Dad was a smoker. Son fought us about going out the window with Adam. I left them and went down the hallway to his parents. Got them out, but the dad was in pretty bad condition."

"I'll try to mention to the investigators that you and Adam were both with the FD at that time. They may swing by the station and want to talk."

I nodded. Anything I could do to help catch this guy. If it was the son, did he blame us for his dad's death? The timeline would match up with his death and when the fires started at the end of last year.

The next three hours crawled at an excruciating pace. It was a few minutes before noon by the time I walked into the hospital lobby. My body lit up when I caught sight of Izzy walking down the long corridor I knew led to the administrative offices.

"You ready?" I asked once she came to a stop in front of me. She nodded. "Yeah."

I stepped to the side, letting her brush past me and placing a hand on the small of her back. Any excuse to touch her, I'd take.

"Any preferences for food?" We only had a few options to choose from since the hospital was located ten minutes outside of town.

"The cafe is always good." She nodded across the street. "Or the diner down the street."

The idea of having her in my truck again, where I could touch her, kiss her, shouldn't send all the blood in my body shooting south, but it did.

"The diner sounds good." I placed my hand on the small of her back once again and turned her toward where I was parked.

Once in the truck, I reached out and placed my hand on her thigh before pulling out into traffic. The second I had the truck in park again, I turned toward her, reaching up to thread my fingers through her hair. Her lips glistened, holding me captive. I leaned forward and brushed my lips gently against hers.

Desire for more engulfed me. I wanted all of her. But right now, it was about spending time with her. Getting to know her more. Showing her I wanted more than strictly the physical stuff. I pulled away and she giggled, reaching up to wipe away the lip gloss she'd left on my face.

"Come on, sweetheart." I grabbed the handle of my door. "Let's go eat."

"I love when you call me that."

"I know." I reached out and tucked her hair behind her ear. "Wait here." I climbed out of the truck and made my way around to her side.

I opened her door and offered her my hand. She eyed it for a moment with a smirk before accepting it. My truck was raised, and although she impressed me when she climbed up in it just fine, with heels on, I wanted to help her down. Really any reason to touch her I would take.

"This place has the best waffles," she said once we were seated in a booth.

"Breakfast for lunch?"

She shrugged. "Why not? I'd eat breakfast anytime of the day. It's my favorite."

I smiled. "Which waffles are your favorite?"

"The Nutella strawberry ones." She peeked at me over her menu. "But I think you'd like the maple bacon one."

"Done." I closed my menu and laid it down.

She cocked an eyebrow. "Wait, I thought you didn't eat carbs and sugars?"

I scoffed. "In the last two and a half weeks, I've eaten pancakes, cookies, donuts, and now waffles. So I'd say what I used to do is no longer relevant."

"The donuts were your idea. I was fine to pass on the pastries that all the kids touched and then put back."

I laughed. "In my defense, I didn't witness that."

The waitress appeared at the table and took our orders. Once she grabbed our menus and walked away, I leaned forward, bracing my forearms on the table.

"Do you like your job at the hospital?"

"Yeah." She nodded, and then her shoulders lifted in a slight shrug. "Sometimes it can get a bit boring, but I like that there are enough tasks to do that I can change it up when I want to."

"But it's only part-time?"

I listened as she explained how she splits the hours with Nicole, and her hope to take over Nicole's hours when she graduates nursing school. The waitress appeared again, delivering our waffles. I couldn't believe how huge they were.

A chuckle slipped through her lips. "Don't worry, I never finish mine."

"This could feed two people." I shook my head and cut off a piece before popping it into my mouth.

"The girls would love these."

I nodded. "Yeah, they would. We should bring them sometime."

Her brows rose enough that I caught it. I wasn't going to correct what I'd said. I wanted to show her what being with me would look like. Occasional lunch dates and breakfast with my kids were part of the package.

"I'd love that." She smiled and forked a piece of her waffle.

My chest suddenly felt tight as an image of the two of us here with Nikki and Alice popped into my head. I could see it so clearly.

Chapter Twenty-Four

IZZY

"He dances...and sings." Logan scoffed. "All the time."

I laughed at his descriptions of Zack, like it was the most ridiculous thing ever, as we walked into the lobby of the hospital. I shot him a sideways look. "Um, I dance too." I knew for a fact I tended to move to music only I could hear.

His lips lifted into the sexiest of smirks before he leaned down, his mouth close to my ear. "Yeah, but I like to watch your ass sway when you dance."

Heat flooded my face as I thought back to the sexy things he'd said to me when he changed my tire. I'd never been with a guy like him. Someone who was so forthcoming in a flirty sort of way.

He straightened and shrugged his shoulders. "I don't find Zack's all that interesting."

I giggled. Never would have thought the grumpy man from that first week would end up being so funny, too.

"About time."

Maggie's voice resonated, and I looked up as she descended the last stair in front of us.

A wide smile broke out on her face as she took the last few steps toward us. "Decided to take my advice, after all?" she directed at Logan.

Logan rolled his eyes. "We grabbed lunch."

"I knew I sensed something last night."

I shifted on my feet, suddenly feeling nervous about how she would feel about this. Logan glanced over at me before turning his attention back to Maggie.

"Don't make her feel uncomfortable."

She sent me a warm smile. "I think it's great." She glanced down quickly at the phone in her hand. "I have surgery in a few, so gotta run."

I let out the breath I was holding once she turned and walked away. I hadn't realized until now that I cared how she would feel about this. But I respected her and appreciated her giving me the opportunity to nanny for them. I still didn't want to do anything to mess it up.

Logan's hand landed on the small of my back again, and my body relaxed.

"You good?"

"Yeah." I tilted my head back to look up at him. "Thank you for lunch."

"Of course. I enjoyed it." His hand fell away, and I instantly missed his touch. "I'll see you tonight."

"Do you mind if I come to soccer practice?"

He raised a brow. "Of course I don't mind. But you sure you don't need that time to yourself before you have to be with them all night?"

I shrugged. It wasn't like they were a handful or anything. I found being with them fun and enjoyable. "They asked me if I would come, and I like watching them play."

He searched my face before his lips lifted into a smile. "Want to come to the house and then ride over with us?"

"Sure." I wasn't sure if he was thinking of the crowded lot or if he wanted me with him. But his grin said he liked my answer.

A moment of awkward silence engulfed us. It was obvious we were both treading lightly, but I didn't care at that moment. I stepped forward and popped up on my tiptoes, pressing my lips against his cheek.

His gaze darkened as he looked down at me, and I didn't miss the way his hand twitched like he wanted to reach out. The fact that I knew he wanted to pull me to him and explore my mouth made my core tighten with anticipation.

"See you this afternoon," he said, taking a step back.

I nodded, and with a final wave, turned toward the corridor that would lead to my office.

The next three hours dragged by. I struggled to focus on anything I needed to do. All I could think about was Logan. The way he kissed me in the front seat of his truck, our date and how he listened so intently, even how my body responded when he placed his hand on the small of my back and leaned down to whisper in my ear.

I was still replaying our date as I made my way through the hospital, ready to get out of there and see Logan again. I shifted impatiently on my heels as I waited for the elevator that would take me down to my car. Finally, the doors opened and I stepped on.

"Hold please," a voice hollered a second before Maggie appeared with a bright smile and jogged through the open doors. "I actually think I'm going to make it to their soccer practice this time."

"They'll be so excited." I knew she was worried she would miss another one. "Is this weird?" I finally asked after a moment. I wasn't one to dance around difficult topics.

Her brows pulled together. "No, why would it be?"

Seriously? Where did I start? "Cause I'm your nanny and now I'm, um... You know, seeing your ex."

She chuckled. "Logan and I have a good relationship. I want him to be happy, and if that's with you, I'm all for it." She huffed. "I mean, it sucks we're going to need to find another nanny. Again. But..." she trailed off as she stared at me.

My face must have given away my surprise, and her expression turned sympathetic.

"Eventually, probably sooner than you realize, you're going to want to spend time alone with Logan when I have the girls. Not have to be at my place."

My shoulders relaxed a hair. I guess she had a point, but I hadn't really thought of that. Was it weird that his ex was the one telling me this?

I shook my head. "You guys have a strange relationship."

"Yes, we've been told that." She sighed. "But we were friends growing up before we ever dated. Just because we weren't good together doesn't mean I don't want him to be happy with someone else."

Nothing in her posture or expression said she wasn't being totally honest. I didn't want this thing with Logan to affect being the girls' nanny. But... if things with Logan became serious, which I hoped was the direction we were going, Maggie was right. They would need to find another nanny, or at least Maggie would.

It all felt so complicated. But my gut said Logan was worth it, and I had to trust in that.

Chapter Twenty-Five

LOGAN

I SMILED as I heard the front door open and the girls ran that way.

"Guess what, Izzy?" Alice asked excitedly.

"What?"

"Mom's coming to soccer practice."

"That's awesome. I bet she can't wait to watch you guys."

I sighed, thinking about my conversation with Maggie on the phone a little bit ago. She apologized and explained what she had said to Izzy. I didn't blame her. It was one of the things being together would mean. Maggie would need to find her own nanny, and that meant Izzy would lose half the hours. She took this job because she needed the money, so I understood that might be an issue for her.

Of course, my first reaction was to fix the situation. But there really wasn't anything I could do to fix this. I'm no idiot. I knew offering to move her in here or pay her bills would not go over well. Izzy was too independent to even consider that. And while I hoped that was where our relationship would eventually lead, I knew it was too soon to start thinking that way. At the moment, the best I could offer was *we'll figure it out*.

The minute she appeared with a smile directed at me, my body relaxed. She didn't seem upset or unsure. Just Izzy. Bright and full of life. It was amazing how her presence could make me feel instantly calm. Ironic, given how a few weeks ago I found her very existence frustrating as hell.

"Alright, girls." I kept my eyes trained on Izzy. "Grab your waters and go get buckled up."

Alice and Nikki snatched their bottles off the kitchen island and headed to the side door that led out to the driveway.

The door shut behind them and I took three steps, stopping in front of Izzy. I tucked a piece of hair behind her ear. "You good?"

She angled her head and studied me.

"Still want to go with us?" I clarified.

Her eyes narrowed slightly, and I bit back a smirk. Damn, she was cute. It was that same glare she sent me when I told her to go home that night I'd changed her tire.

"I already told you I want to."

I nodded and opened my mouth to respond, but she spoke again before I could.

"I rarely change my mind when I decide I want something." Her eyebrows rose slightly before she added, "Or want to do something."

I gathered she wasn't only talking about going to soccer practice. I couldn't stop the smile that lifted my lips.

"Alright. Let's go then, sweetheart."

I followed her out the door, trying and failing to not stare at her ass in another pair of tiny cutoffs. The ride to the field was torture. I wanted to reach over and hold her hand, or rest my hand on her thigh. I settled for resting my arm on the center console so my pinkie could brush along her arm.

Soccer practice went smoothly. The girls did well, and Maggie and Izzy spent most of it chatting. It was nice that they got along. Most people who got divorced rarely got along, let alone with their exes' significant others.

What sucked was when we got back to the house and I had to gather my stuff and head to work. I hugged both of my girls and waited until they disappeared into the great room before I nodded toward the front foyer.

Izzy followed behind me, and I turned to her once we were alone in the small space at the front of the house. She let out a giggle as I pulled her into a hug and buried my nose in her hair. Strawberries were quickly becoming my favorite scent.

"I'll text you later."

She nodded and tilted back to look up at me. "Okay."

I pressed my lips to her forehead and then forced myself to turn and walk out the door.

Almost immediately when I arrived at the house and settled in, the alarms went off. A car accident and a report of a possible gas leak right after finishing up with the wreck had us busy for three hours.

Once back at the house, Terri, one of our EMTs, and Kyle got pulled back out on a cardiac arrest call while the rest of us gathered in the common area. I filled them in about what Dylan had told me earlier.

"A kid?" Jay asked.

I narrowed my eyes at him. "Not a fucking kid. He's old enough to know better."

"Chill." He glared back. "I just meant it's a young guy. Not even fucking old enough to drink yet. He's around my sister's age."

I wasn't about to point out she wasn't a kid either. That would open another can of worms I wanted to avoid.

"I definitely remember him," Adam jumped in, always the peacekeeper. "Like from the fire seven years ago. He kept refusing to listen to me, intent on going to help his parents."

I nodded, remembering how defiant and stubborn he had been. And while I understood how traumatic the whole thing must have been, it didn't give him a pass from intentionally setting fires. I hoped they found something that would lead to an arrest soon. Or at the very least scare him into stopping.

We chatted some more about the situation before everyone dispersed for the night. Adam and Jay started a game of rummy, while Seth and Zack went to the bunk room to try to sleep for a bit before another call came in.

I relaxed back in the recliner and pulled up my text thread with Izzy. I couldn't believe how much I missed her. I bit back a chuckle at the difference from a few weeks ago to now. I'd gone from avoiding her like the fucking plague to missing her presence when I wasn't with her.

> Me: Girls asleep?

> Izzy: Yeah. You guys have been busy. Heard the alarms go off like twice now since you left.

> Me: Yeah. It's probably going to be one of those nights.

> Me: What are you doing?

> Izzy: Watching Yellowjackets.

> Me: Wish I was there.

> Izzy: Me too...cuddle while we watch TV.

> Me: You probably wear tiny-ass sleep shorts, don't you?

> Izzy: *Picture of her legs with just a hint of pink satin shorts*

A groan bubbled up, and I swallowed it back down. Didn't need or want to draw attention to myself.

> Me: Ugh. I'd probably do a shit job of keeping my hands to myself.

> Izzy: If you were here I wouldn't want you to keep your hands to yourself.

> Me: I'd pull you onto my lap like in the truck last night. Watching you move against me has been on repeat in my head.

> Izzy: 😳 😊

I could feel eyes burning a hole through me, and I set my phone down before glancing over to the kitchen area. Adam and Jay were shooting daggers my way. More so Jay than Adam. My guess for different reasons. Adam, because I didn't take his advice yet. But Jay made it clear he didn't want me dating his sister. I understood why. That didn't mean I was going to listen. Izzy needed to make her own decision.

Regardless, it didn't make any sense to have that conversation with him yet. Not until I was sure where things were going with her. I wanted to be confident that she wanted the same things I did, but it was hard to wrap my head around being a young twenty-one-year-old and wanting to date someone who not only worked weird hours but was also a single parent.

I needed to shut my brain down and try to get a few hours of sleep. I had a feeling tonight was going to be a long one. The trick to not being exhausted by the end of a night shift was to try to sleep as much as possible between calls.

I typed out one last message to Izzy.

Me: Goodnight sweetheart.

Izzy: Goodnight Logan.

Chapter Twenty-Six

LOGAN

COMING HOME and spotting Izzy moving around the kitchen to her own beat, swaying to music that blasted loudly from her phone, was the best. Never did I think loud and chaotic to be something I'd crave, but here we were. It was impossible to avoid getting swept up in her energy.

"Daddy," Alice bolted my way.

I lifted her into my arms and moved further into the kitchen.

"Want to help us make French toast?"

I chuckled. "Sure."

The smirk Izzy sent me would have me agreeing to anything. "Hope you don't freak out when they get egg everywhere."

Wait. Was she serious?

"Chillax." She giggled. "I was only kidding. It's usually only a little bit of egg."

My facial expression must have given away my disgust.

"And I'll clean it right up. Promise."

I shook my head. Jesus, what had I gotten myself into. But I came around the island and helped dip the pieces of bread into the egg mixture, then handed the plate to Izzy to toss onto the griddle. Ten minutes, and a surprisingly minimal amount of mess later, the girls were happily eating their French toast.

"I'll pick them up from school again," I said, leaning back against the counter and crossing one ankle over the other.

She nodded. "Okay. Did you want me to drop them off so you can head to bed?"

Wanting to take her to bed ran through my mind, but I couldn't say that, so I gave her a clipped nod instead. "Yeah. If you don't mind, that'd be great."

"Not at all."

I was amazed at how much of a smooth routine she had down and how well the girls knew it, too. They were running upstairs with instructions to get dressed and brush their teeth as soon as they finished eating, while Izzy finished packing lunches and put them in their backpacks.

Finally, I couldn't stand it anymore. Pushing away from the counter, I grabbed her hand and pulled her toward me. Tangling my fingers in her hair, I pressed my lips against hers, parting them with my tongue and savoring the way she melted into my embrace.

I broke the kiss and rested my forehead on hers. "I missed you."

"Me too." She sighed. "Two more nights of this?"

I chuckled even as fresh worry bubbled up now that she saw how sucky the hours could be. But I nodded. "Yeah, tonight and tomorrow night. And then I'm off for a few days."

"That'll be nice."

We stood like that until we heard two sets of feet bounding down the stairs.

She stepped back and smiled. "See you tonight, papa bear."

I growled, and she sent me a wink before turning toward the girls and ushering them out the door.

Then it was quiet. No noise or chaos. And I hated it.

Chapter Twenty-Seven

IZZY

THE LAST TWENTY-FOUR hours kind of sucked. I couldn't lie about that. I worked at the hospital yesterday after dropping the twins off at school. Then I was back at Logan's by six, but he had to leave early because of a large house fire that needed more guys. So I literally only got to see him for a few minutes.

I glanced at the time on my phone, hoping he would be home soon. The girls were still sleeping. It was a Saturday, so no need to wake them, and I probably kept them up a little too late last night. But I'd texted Logan to make sure a movie and popcorn until eleven was fine.

The side door opened, and I immediately started moving toward him. He didn't miss a beat as he dropped his bag and his hands grasped my waist before he pulled me flush against his body. My core throbbed as his tongue thrust into my mouth, teasing, exploring. There was so much need in this kiss. So much desire. I'd never experienced anything like this before, and I wanted more. More of this. More of him.

He pulled back, his gaze so dark and needy, likely mirroring my own.

"Assuming girls are still sleeping?"

I nodded and he grabbed me by my ass and lifted me. I wrapped my legs around his waist and he turned, pressing me back against the wall.

"Good." His lips found mine again.

He rotated his hips, rubbing his hard cock along my clit. I broke the kiss and let my head fall back against the wall with a moan.

"Shh." He moved again. "You need to be quiet, sweetheart."

His lips brushed along the column of my throat where my pulse pounded hard. He continued to swivel his hips, grinding against me as he licked and sucked the sensitive skin of my neck.

"Logan." I pressed my teeth into my bottom lip, attempting to quiet my moans. Jesus, I wasn't sure how much more I could take. The need to be with him was so overwhelming, I wasn't even sure I could form words.

"What is it you want?"

"You. I want you."

He spun suddenly, still holding me to him, and took two steps before bracing me on the edge of the kitchen table. "Can you be quiet?"

Oh, fuck yes. I nodded and pressed my teeth harder into my lip. I wasn't sure what he had in mind. I doubted he planned to have me right here with his kids asleep upstairs. But his gaze was all sorts of serious, and I'd agree to just about anything if it meant I could feel him. His touch. His mouth. Any of him.

He glanced down at my sleep shorts and groaned. "Do these even cover your ass."

I smirked. "Mostly."

He slowly looked back up my body as his fingers danced along the hem of my shorts. I braced my hands behind me and leaned back, giving him more access.

"You like teasing me?" His thumb disappeared under the fabric of my shorts and pressed hard against my clit.

My hips bucked, and his grip tightened on my hip, holding me still.

"I like the way you look at me."

"And how do I look at you?"

I stared at him, trying to find the right words to describe it. "Like you couldn't possibly go another minute without kissing me. Or touching me."

"That is very accurate." He smiled. "Even if you were wearing sweats that covered your gorgeous body, I'd still want to touch you. To feel your lips against mine." He pushed the fabric of my panties to the side before running his thumb through my wetness. "Jesus. You're soaked, sweetheart. This all for me?"

I nodded, although he knew the answer to that. "I've never been so turned on in my life."

His lips lifted into a cocky smirk.

"Logan, please." My body was vibrating with need.

"Please, what?" His thumb continued to move up and down. "You want me to make you come?"

"Yes." I pulled my lip all the way into my mouth. "Please. I can't—"

He pushed two fingers deep inside me, cutting off my words as I fought to keep quiet. Finally, he was no longer teasing me as he slid his fingers in and out of me, working me over until I was panting and moaning.

He growled as his hand holding onto my hip slid up my back and pulled me forward. His mouth slammed down on mine, and he swallowed down my moans as his other hand continued to bring me closer and closer to the edge.

My body pulsed with pleasure as my core tightened and my orgasm tore through me. His movements slowed and he removed his hand, pulling back enough so he could press his lips to my forehead.

"Such a good girl," he murmured. "Next time it'll be my mouth making you come."

I sagged into his hold, and his arms tightened around me. We lived in that quiet moment until the sound of little feet came from upstairs. I wasn't ready for this interlude with him to end, but this probably wasn't the way he wanted to tell the girls about us.

He stepped back, and I slid my feet to the floor. He searched my face, longing still blazing in his gaze. Finally, Alice and Nikki twirled into the kitchen like mini tornados.

I moved further into the kitchen. "Okay you two, pancakes, waffles, or French toast?"

"Waffles," Alice exclaimed.

"French toast," Nikki countered.

I smiled at them and shook my head. This wasn't the first time we'd had this issue. "You know my rule."

They turned toward each other and put out their little fists. "Rock, paper, scissors, shoot."

"Scissors cut paper." Alice smiled proudly.

I glanced over at Logan. "Are you heading to bed or joining us?"

"I'll wait and eat breakfast. I'm suddenly starving." His lips lifted into the sexiest smirk I'd seen him wear so far.

"Really?" I dragged the word out and matched his smirk with one of my own.

"But Dad, you don't eat waffles."

"That is true. But you and Izzy make the best. I can't possibly pass them up. I am going to make some scrambled eggs, though. Who wants some with their waffles?"

"Me," both girls said in unison.

Logan stepped up to the sink and washed his hands with another sexy smirk aimed at me. The reminder of what we just did caused my body to come alive with need all over again. I still didn't understand how one look from him was all it took.

The four of us worked together in the kitchen, prepping the eggs and waffles. I struggled to keep my gaze from continuing to drift to Logan helping his girls. He was so good with them, even when it was obvious letting them make a mess was not easy for him. It all felt so domestic, and I loved it. I understood the responsibility that came with having a family, but I wanted him to know, to see, this could be the kind of life I'd find joy in. I didn't see the twins as a negative thing, but an added bonus.

He carried over the bowl of beaten eggs and waffle batter. Standing next to him at the stove, I started pouring the batter into the waffle pan as he began scrambling the eggs.

"Would it be okay if I take the girls to the spring festival in town after breakfast?"

He studied me for a heartbeat before his lips lifted into a small smile that had my belly fluttering again.

"Yeah, that's fine," he said with a slight nod of his head. "Or if you wanted to wait, we could go together. I only need a few hours of sleep and I'll be good."

"You sure?" He didn't need to offer that. He could totally have a kid-free house for a few hours, or rest and then take them himself, but was it dumb to hope his offer meant he wanted to spend more time with me too?

He leaned over, his warm breath close to my ear sending a shiver racing down my spine. "I like spending time with you, sweetheart. So yes, I'm sure."

Warmth blossomed in my chest, spreading through my body, and I turned slightly to look at him. Our gazes met, and when his drifted down to my lips, my breath caught. Only a few inches lay between us, and I wanted so badly to kiss him again.

Giggling erupted from the other side of the island, and we both turned our gazes toward the girls.

"Are you guys gonna kiss?" Nikki asked as her nose scrunched.

Logan paused and surveyed them thoughtfully. "Would you think that was weird?"

Nikki shrugged. "Jesse kisses Mom. She says when two people really like each other, they kiss."

"And you really like Izzy," Alice added with a wide smile.

He chuckled and glanced back at me. "I do *really* like Izzy."

Heat spread up my neck and into my face. I pulled my gaze away and focused back on the waffles, turning the pan over. Willing my face to turn back to its normal shade.

As we sat at the table together and ate, we told the girls about taking them to the festival. They were so excited, as soon as they finished their waffles, they took their plates to the sink and ran upstairs to get dressed.

"I don't think they realize we're not going until after you wake up." I stood with my plate in my hands.

He chuckled. "I don't think they do either. You still okay with that plan?"

"Of course." The fact that we were going to do this together, the four of us, made me so utterly happy. I reached over to grab his plate and a sudden whiff of charred wood hit me. I leaned closer to his hair, breathing him in.

A chuckle left his lips. "Did you just smell me? I mean, I smell you all the time because you smell like strawberries. But I probably still stink from my quick shower this morning."

"You don't stink." I shook my head. "I love the way you smell. It's the smoke." How did I explain this? I shrugged. "Reminds me of my father, my childhood. I find it comforting, familiar. I don't know, it probably sounds stupid." I could already feel my face heating.

He stared at me for so long I felt the need to squirm.

"Not stupid." His fingers trailed up the back of my leg leaving gooseflesh in their wake. "I love that. Love that you can find comfort in something I can give you."

There went those damn butterflies again.

"Go sleep. So we can go to the festival." I leaned down and

brushed my lips quickly against his before moving toward the sink.

He headed up to bed, and by the time I finished cleaning up the kitchen, the girls were playing quietly with Legos in the great room. I told them I'd be right back and went upstairs to change.

I loved the flowy tank top and cutoffs I brought for today, and when Logan entered the great room an hour later and his heated gaze skimmed over my body, it was obvious he did too.

As we rode in his truck to the festival, he entwined our hands, bringing mine to his lips and placing a chaste kiss on the back. I glanced at the girls in the back as they giggled. I loved how simple the whole thing was. Even when he won them both a stuffed bear at a carnival game, they told him he had to get one for me, too.

"Of course, I have to win my girl a prize."

His girl. The sheer happiness those words evoked was indescribable.

Chapter Twenty-Eight

LOGAN

As SOON AS we got back to the house, Nikki and Alice darted out back to play on the swing set. How did they still have energy after spending three hours walking around the festival?

"Why don't I stay at this point?" Izzy handed me a glass of sweet tea she'd just poured and then took the seat next to me at the kitchen table. "I can make dinner."

I glanced at my watch. It was almost five. She would need to be back here in less than two hours. At least this was my last night shift scheduled for a bit.

"You sure?" I raised a brow at her. "You don't have to if you need a break." As much as I wanted her here, I wanted her to know I understood she had her own life and responsibilities.

"I want to be here." She looked down at her glass as she

tapped her fingers on the side of it. "Unless you want it to be you and the girls for a bit. I totally understand—"

I grabbed her hand and threaded my fingers through hers. She raised her gaze to meet mine. "Having you here. Making waffles and going to the festival. It was perfect. So yeah, I want you to stay."

"Good," she said with a smile.

We sat there holding hands and watching Alice and Nikki play out the back window until Izzy got up and headed into the kitchen to start prepping dinner. I offered to order something, but she wanted to cook. And the next few hours flew by. Watching the girls help Izzy make dinner, sitting at the table together eating, and now playing Clue Junior—it all made me hate the idea that I had to leave.

I glanced down at my watch, not believing another twenty minutes had gone by. Time was inching closer and closer to seven.

"What time do you have to go in?" Izzy asked.

"I told them I'd be in after the girls go to bed, but technically I'm on call starting at seven." I'd planned to do the same thing last night, but got called in a little after Izzy had gotten here.

We played another round of Clue, and then it was Nikki's turn to pick something. That turned into two rounds of the Disney version of Chutes and Ladders.

Once the games were cleaned up, I checked my watch again. "Alright, girls." I wanted to be able to read them a story before I was called in. "Let's get you two in bed and I'll read you a story."

Luckily, they were already in their pajamas and had brushed their teeth before we started the games. After they said goodnight to Izzy, I followed them upstairs. Three books later, I gave them each a kiss and pulled the door shut behind me as I left the room.

I found Izzy curled up at one end of the couch, her legs tucked up next to her. Desperate to feel her lips again, I stalked toward her, bracing my hands on either side of her before claiming her mouth. As my tongue explored, she sat up on her knees and wrapped her arms around my neck. Her little moans took me back to earlier, when she came all over my hand. Instantly hard, my dick pushed against the fabric of my pants, begging to be set free.

She pulled back, her breath coming in shallow gasps, questions in her eyes. She could obviously feel my need for her pressing against her stomach.

"Logan...I..."

"I know, sweetheart." I pressed my lips to her forehead. "Me too. But I'm not starting something with you that we might not be able to finish tonight. I want to take my time with you, and then be able to hold you all night."

She pushed her bottom lip out into a pout, once again reminding me of that night I changed her tire. But just like that night, I found her adorable.

I placed a kiss on her nose. "You're cute."

She cocked her head. "Cute?"

"Yes. When you pout. I think it's cute."

My phone blared loudly, the tones reminding me I had to go. I didn't want to, but I had to. She continued to pout, but nothing in her body language said she was overly upset that I had to go. It was a relief to know she was getting to see what my life was like, and so far it didn't bother her.

I pressed another quick kiss to her forehead. "Gotta go."

She nodded and followed me to the door, gifting me one more quick kiss before I walked to my truck and drove toward the station.

Chapter Twenty-Nine

IZZY

SPENDING the night without Logan was super hard, especially knowing he wanted me as much as I did him. But tonight was his last night shift, then he'd be off for a few days, and tomorrow Maggie would have the twins back. So there was nothing stopping us from being together. At least as far as I knew.

I glanced in the living room where the girls were sitting, watching a show. I'd already fed them breakfast, and it was after eight. The guys must have gotten a call they were stuck on given Logan wasn't home yet.

I'd just finished cleaning the kitchen from breakfast when the sound of his truck pulling down the driveway hit my ears. Excitement coursed through me as I spun toward the side door. The moment he stepped inside, our gazes locked, and a smile lifted his lips. My stomach flipped as he kept his heated stare trained on me. But in his gaze was something else, too. Something more.

"Daddy's home," Alice announced from the great room.

He headed into the large open space and listened to the girls chatter about their show. His gaze drifted over to me more than once, almost like he was checking if I was still there.

After another few minutes, he turned toward me and made his way around the kitchen island where I was leaning back against the countertop. He mimicked my stance next to me and entwined our fingers together. Jesus, just that simple touch had need pooling in my belly.

"So, what's the plan today?" I swallowed and tried to focus on our conversation and not the way my body responded to his touch.

"Maggie should be here around two to pick them up if you can hang out until then. I'm going to spend some time with them before heading to bed."

"Okay." I nodded. That was what I thought, but I needed something to take my mind off the fluttering in my belly.

"Can I take you out tonight?"

My core throbbed from anticipation of what that could mean. "Like on a date?" A date that could end in his bed since he wouldn't have the girls here, he was off, and I wasn't needed at Maggie's until tomorrow morning.

"Yeah, a date." He unlaced our fingers and ran one knuckle up the inside of my arm. "Anywhere you want to go."

Sensations shot through my body, starting with the path his finger made up and down my arm, and landing between my thighs. I squeezed my legs together and pulled my bottom lip into my mouth, fighting the urge to tell him I didn't care where we went as long as it ended with me spending the night with him.

"I love sitting on the back patio area of The Dock." The view of the lake was breathtaking.

"Sounds perfect." He leaned down close to my ear. "Wherever you choose will be perfect, as long as I'm there with you."

He laced our fingers together once more and tugged me closer as he leaned back and laid a quick kiss on my forehead. Warmth spread through my chest and up my neck as a feeling of utter happiness settled deep in my soul.

After he'd spent a little bit more time with the twins, he went upstairs to bed. I had to admit the thought of climbing in with him after Maggie picked up the girls a few hours later crossed my mind. But I wanted tonight to be special. To wear something that would drive him crazy with lust, so there was no way he could resist. Not that I thought he would.

Heading back to my apartment, I stood in the middle of my bedroom and picked up my phone, opening my text thread with Nicole and the girls.

> Me: He's taking me on a date tonight. What should I wear?

Mia: Depends. You want this to end with sex?

Lyla: Can you show us options?

I laid three dresses out on my bed and snapped a picture.

Nicole: The black one will be super easy to get out of 😉

The short dress tied around the neck and was cut low in the back.

Lyla: The blue is really pretty though. But the halter will probably drive him insane.

Nicole: How did yesterday go?

> Me: Well... we kinda fooled around in the kitchen before the kids woke up.

Lyla: Oh my.

Me: It was so freaking hot. Then we took them to the festival and he called me his girl.

Lyla: Definitely the black one! He'll spend the whole night desperate for you and it'll make afterwards so much hotter!

Nicole: I agree. Unless you don't want to have sex with him yet.

Me: I want him so bad I haven't been able to think about anything else.

Mia: Go with the halter. Don't wear a bra.

Images of him untying my dress and lowering his mouth to my nipples caused a moan to bubble up and slip through my lips.

Waiting three more hours to see his reaction was going to be the worst kind of torture.

Chapter Thirty

LOGAN

"Right this way." The young hostess turned and began walking through the main dining room of The Dock.

I placed my hand on Izzy's lower back as we followed. The sexy dress she wore had been torturing me since the moment she opened her door. I wanted nothing more in that moment than to pull her against me and slide my hands up under the short skirt. Make her come with my fingers like I did yesterday morning. Hear her little moans echo off the walls.

The need that had consumed me so many times over the last few days was unlike anything I'd experienced. I kept my gaze trained on her as she took her seat, unable to look away. We both wanted the same thing tonight, that was obvious. But I also didn't want to take it that far if she wasn't sure about us.

"Logan?"

I shook my head, realizing I was standing there staring at her like a weirdo. "Sorry."

"You okay?"

"Yep." I took the seat across from her and laid my hand palm up on the small table. "You're so beautiful, I can't help but stare sometimes."

Her cheeks tinged pink as she put her hand in mine, and I ran my thumb back and forth along the back of it.

She pulled her bottom lip between her teeth, and it was so fucking sexy, a groan slipped through my lips. I wanted to reach up and pull it out and then replace it with my thumb. Or, better yet, my cock.

But that would have to wait. For now, I'd enjoy the torturous game of flirting we were playing.

After the waitress came and took our order, we were alone once again.

"The lake is gorgeous."

I followed her gaze out to the line of mountains in the distance where the sun was setting behind the peaks. The blends of orange, pink, and yellow in the sky did make for a picture-perfect scene.

"It is." Although I agreed with her, she was the one I couldn't stop looking at. "Do you like being on the water?"

"Yeah, we've rented canoes and small boats over the years."

"I want to buy a boat eventually." It was one of the things my mom had argued I should use my trust for, even though I kept telling her I wasn't touching it.

"Really?" She cocked her head to the side. "Aren't those like really expensive?"

I shifted uncomfortably. Firefighters' salaries weren't substantial, but since Maggie made a lot more money than I did, we ended up paying off the house, and I got it in the divorce. Not having a mortgage payment allowed me to have more freedom financially. But it still wasn't an unlimited well of funds. Definitely not boat money.

"Yeah. It's probably just a pipe dream." But I hoped, as I continued to save, it was something I could afford one day. With a shrug, I added, "But the girls have liked it the few times I rented one."

I brushed my thumb over the back of her hand again and smiled when I felt her shiver with need. She was so fucking responsive to my touch. Every damn time. It was utter perfection.

Her mouth opened slightly and her breathing sped up, her chest rising and falling more rapidly. "Do you, I mean what do..." she paused and shifted in her seat "...you guys do over the summer? Do you, ummm, take the girls anywhere?"

I smirked, loving the way my touch was affecting her. "I usually rent some Airbnb somewhere on the coast."

She leaned forward and braced her arm on the table. I trailed my gaze from her face down the column of her neck before ending at her tits, now pushed up into the deep V of her dress. Images of pulling her around the table and making her sit on my lap as I reached up and untied her dress inundated me. My cock hardened and pushed uncomfortably against the zipper of my pants. I adjusted myself and looked back up, meeting her eyes.

A sexy, knowing smile lifted her lips and I shifted forward, tugging her hand and causing her to lean closer.

"That dress has been driving me crazy since you opened your door." Not that I needed to tell her that, but I wanted to. Wanted to watch her blush and squirm.

"Oh?" Her cheeks turned a light shade of pink. "How so?"

"The only thing preventing me from taking it off you is that string around your neck." I smirked. "And I can't stop wondering what you're wearing underneath."

"I guess you'll have to wait and find out." She pulled her bottom lip between her teeth again, and her pupils blew out.

"I definitely plan on finding out."

Our gazes stayed locked for a long moment, only broken when the waitress appeared with our food.

Reluctantly, I let go of her hand and leaned back in my seat, allowing the server to place our plates down. Suddenly, I had no interest in eating, only in laying Izzy out and feasting on her.

The next twenty minutes crawled by as we ate and chatted, sharing heated looks. The tension between us grew as each minute passed by. I slid my credit card into the black check holder, and when the waitress stepped back up to the table, I thrust it at her, desperate to be alone with Izzy.

I turned my attention back to her as she pulled her hair to the side, draping it over one shoulder and exposing the slender column of her neck. I shifted uncomfortably for probably the hundredth time since we first got in the truck together when I picked her up.

Finished with the check, we stood and I laid my hand on the small of her back as we made our way through the restaurant. Her body shivered under my touch, and I couldn't stop my hand from moving up her back until it met bare skin.

Opening the passenger side door, I gave her a hand up into her seat. The skirt of her dress rode up, and I wasn't sure if she did it on purpose, but her legs opened slightly, giving me a peek of bright pink panties.

"Logan." My name was barely a whisper on her lips.

I trailed my gaze back up her body until I locked eyes with her. Desire and need swam in her irises. I knew what she wanted. The same thing I did. But I also wanted her to tell me.

"What do you want, sweetheart?"

"You." She let her legs fall open a little wider. "Your touch, your lips...all of it."

I ran one hand up her outer thigh, stopping at the hem of her dress. "You sure?"

"I've never been so sure of anything as much as I'm sure about this."

"If you stay in my bed tonight,"—I inched my hand further

up her thigh—"there's no going back for me. So if you need more time…"

"No." She gripped my hand and squeezed. "You're what I want. This is what I want." She moved my hand over until my thumb brushed her soaked panties. "Take me home, Logan."

As I moved my thumb back and forth over the outside of the fabric, she gripped my shoulders. I removed my hand and stepped back, openly adjusting myself. I wanted her to see exactly how she affected me.

Shutting her door, I made my way around the truck. I held her hand as I drove us back to my house. If I touched her thigh again, felt her soaked panties, or heard her little moans, I wasn't sure we would even make it back to the house. The Dock was only a five-minute drive, but it felt so much longer.

The minute we stepped into the house and I shut the door behind us, she spun toward me, stepping back with a seductive glint in her eyes. As if her movements were in slow motion, she reached up and pulled the strap behind her neck loose.

The black fabric fell, exposing her gorgeous tits, and gathered around her waist. Her nipples were hard peaks, the color reminding me of her cheeks whenever she blushed. I licked my lips, desperate to get them in my mouth. Desperate to taste her. To make her scream out my name.

"I want to see all of you. Every single inch that I've only fantasized about." I tipped my head toward the clothing that still covered her. "Take the rest off, sweetheart."

Her eyes darkened, the green of her irises almost nonexistent. Using the palms of her hands, she shimmied the black material of the dress over her hips until it fell down her legs and piled on the floor.

She stood in front of me in only a tiny pink thong and black heels. My dick hardened until it was almost painful as I raked my gaze over her body. I took two steps toward her and reached out, letting my thumb brush back and forth over her hard nipple. Her teeth pressed into her bottom lip, and little sounds of pleasure slipped out.

I gripped her hip with my other hand and pulled her close, eliminating all the space between us. "Feel that?"

She nodded and palmed me through my pants. "I need you."

Just that touch alone sent me close to the edge. I wanted to make her feel good. Give her what she needed first, because I had no idea how long I'd last once I got inside her.

Gripping her hips, I spun and backed her against the wall. My mouth dropped to hers, our tongues colliding in a frenzied need. I cupped one breast and flicked my thumb across her pebbled nipple. The moan that vibrated through her was so intense I could feel it under my touch.

I moved my hand up under her jaw and wrapped it around the front of her neck, tilting her head back. She arched into me as I licked a path down her throat, her moans intensifying as my lips wrapped around one sensitive peak.

"You like that?" I moved across her breasts, lavishing the same attention on the other one.

"Yes," she panted.

Getting down on my knees, I kissed my way down her belly and hooked my fingers under the waistband of her thong. Like a present I'd been waiting to unwrap, I slowly dragged it down her legs. Lifting her foot up, I trailed kisses up her calf and placed it over my shoulder.

Pinning her with my gaze, I leaned forward and took one long lap. Her creamy skin was flushed pink and her back bowed with each flick I took of her clit. I slid one finger into her warm, wet pussy as I licked up every drop of her.

"More. I need more," she breathed out, grinding her pussy into my face. "There. Right there."

I added another finger, stretching her, and then sucked hard. Her thighs trembled as I flicked the tip of my tongue against her one last time. She exploded, her body shaking violently as she came.

Fuck. I needed to be inside her more than I needed my next breath. I stood and grabbed her by the ass, lifting her and carrying her up the stairs.

"We need a bed." I wanted to spend all night showing her how she made me feel. Feeling her wrapped around my cock.

She giggled and ran her lips down my neck. The sensation shot through my body as I entered my bedroom and laid her down on the bed. Blonde curls framed out around her, and using the tip of my finger, I brushed a piece away from her face.

Jesus Christ. I swallowed as I stared down at her spread out, completely naked and ready for me. Full pink lips that glistened and parted as she gazed back at me. Intense green eyes still hooded from pleasure. Creamy skin flushed a luscious pink.

"You're beautiful, sweetheart." Although I was desperate to feel her, I wanted to savor this moment with her. It all felt so intense. More intense than I'd ever experienced, and I had no idea what to make of that.

That feeling escalated as she tracked my movements. Reaching behind me with one hand, I pulled my shirt over my head. Her gaze trailed over my chest, and she ran her tongue along her bottom lip as she soaked me in, continuing to track my movements as I discarded the rest of my clothing.

The mattress dipped as I climbed onto the bed and knelt between her legs.

She ran her hand up my stomach and chest. "You make me feel beautiful. The way you look at me isn't like anything I've experienced. Not ever."

"Good. I want to be the only guy who's ever made you feel that way." I fisted my cock in my hand and ran the tip through her wetness. Our gazes locked. "And now you're mine."

She smiled. "Yours."

A growl slipped through my lips as I fought the urge to thrust deep inside her. I shifted back. "Need to grab a condom."

Her hands shot out and gripped my biceps. "Logan. I'm on the pill."

So much desire and vulnerability swam in her gaze it punched me right in the chest. The fact that she trusted me to take her bare left me with an intense feeling of need. Both physical and emotional.

"You sure?"

She nodded. "Please. I want to feel you."

"I want that too," I whispered, slowly crawling up her body until I hovered above her. "More than you know." As I inched slowly inside her, feeling her walls squeezing around me, I knew I wouldn't last long. Pleasure shot down my spine with each inch. "Jesus," I hissed.

She raised her hips and I sank the rest of the way in. A groan left my lips and her eyes flicked up to mine, holding me captive, her mouth parted as she adjusted to my size.

Her fingers dug into my back. "Need you to move."

I lost the ability to think. Or form words. This exact moment, as I filled her to the hilt, was everything I'd been waiting months for. Her pussy clenching around me finally got me moving. I dragged my cock all the way out before slamming forward into her. With every thrust, she lifted her hips until I was grinding against her swollen clit.

"Right there." She dragged her nails down my back before digging them into my ass. "Harder."

I lifted her leg over my hip and rocked harder into her, rotating my hips with each thrust.

Her walls gripped me like a vice, and I couldn't hold out any longer. She felt too damn good. I'd spend all night making it up to her. Thankfully, her body shook, and the cry of pleasure that slipped from her lips sent us over the edge together.

My mouth crashed down on hers, molding together as I continued to move in and out of her, pulling every ounce of pleasure from both of us. Completely and utterly spent, I collapsed down on top of her. After giving myself a second to catch my breath, I rolled us so she was tucked into my side.

"We're going to do that again." I smirked and pressed my lips to the top of her head. "Might need to give this old man time to recover, though."

She swatted my stomach playfully. "Oh stop, you're not old."

Maybe not. But I knew one thing. I needed to make my daily workouts a priority now. Because I wanted to spend every night exactly like this.

Chapter Thirty-One

IZZY

My ALARM SOUNDED from somewhere nearby, and I buried my head deeper into the warm, hard pillow, simultaneously struggling to understand why it felt so hard but so comfortable at the same time. My eyelids fluttered open as a deep rumble came from above my head. I smiled, the night before coming back to me instantly, and I ran my hand up Logan's tight abs through the dusting of hair that led to a larger patch covering his chest. This time a sexy groan slipped through his lips.

Being with him was unlike anything I'd ever experienced. His intense focus on every detail. How he took his time, not rushing through the moments but stretching them out and making me desperate for more.

"Sweetheart, if you keep that up, I'm gonna end up making you late."

I froze. The reason my alarm had gone off finally hit me. I had to be at Maggie's this morning. Her words ran through my head. Ultimately, she was right. I wanted to be here with him.

His chest rumbled again, and he shifted, rolling us so he hovered above me.

"What's wrong?"

"How will this work?" I searched his face. "Like with the nanny thing."

"We'll figure it out." He leaned down and brushed his lips gently over mine before pulling back to look at me. "I know one thing. I want as much time with you as I can get. I'm a very needy, selfish man." His lips lifted slightly.

I rolled my eyes. The way he focused on what I needed last night instead of his own needs made that statement ridiculous.

He tilted forward and pressed a quick kiss to my forehead. "Most likely, the solution will be Maggie needing her own nanny. I don't share well."

I chuckled. "You didn't even want me as the nanny."

"Because I knew it would be harder to ignore the way you made me feel if I was around you all the time."

"And now?" Jesus. Apparently, I was the needy one—needing to hear him say he didn't regret this.

A growl tumbled from his lips, and his hand came up to cup my face. "Sweetheart, look at me."

I met his gaze, and in it swirled no indecision, just unbridled truth.

"I'm so fucking glad you said yes to Maggie. That you called me that night you got the flat. That over the last few weeks you've become important to not only the girls but to me too. I don't regret a single moment. Okay?"

I swallowed and nodded. Every time I thought he couldn't possibly surprise me, he did.

His lips met mine, and I sagged back into the mattress as his tongue explored my mouth until my alarm went off again.

He groaned. "I guess you can't ignore that one again."

I shook my head. "No. I really need to get ready to go."

"Fine." He huffed dramatically and rolled off me. "If you must."

I giggled. He was so playful at times, it was hard to imagine I ever thought he was grumpy. I could feel his eyes on me as I climbed out of the bed and headed toward the attached bathroom. With a quick glance over my shoulder, I paused in the doorway. He leaned up on his elbows, his heated gaze raking over my naked body.

"Come back over after you drop the girls off at school."

I raised an eyebrow. "And what if I said no?"

His lips twitched. "You won't."

"So confident?"

"Yes. Because good girls get rewarded."

My cheeks heated. "And what is my reward?"

"Making you come on my tongue over and over until you're begging me to stop."

I squeezed my legs together to ease the tension his words caused.

The corner of his lips pulled up. "You better hurry."

Excitement zipped through my body as I turned and disappeared into the bathroom. I'd never felt this way about anyone I'd dated. And although I didn't know how it was going to work out, I had faith we would figure it out together.

Chapter Thirty-Two

LOGAN

Thinking about the last few days with Izzy made me smile. We'd spent every minute we could together. After the way Nikki and Alice responded to the idea that I was going to kiss Izzy on Saturday, I wasn't really worried about how they would react to us being together. But I knew they would have questions. They'd both giggled this morning when I kissed Izzy on the cheek before leaving for work. It felt so natural and so right, I didn't even give myself a moment to think about it. Starting tonight, the girls would be with Maggie for the next five days. And I planned to make the most of it with Izzy.

I stepped back and inspected the rig, pride surging through me. I loved giving it a fresh wash. Voices echoed from inside the

AJ RANNEY

bay, and I glanced that way. Seth stood, arms crossed, glowering at Zack, who was dancing around like a kid on Christmas morning.

"The probie smiled," Zack announced loudly, pointing toward Seth. "It was real quick, but he smiled."

I shook my head. Seth had slowly acclimated to us over the last couple of weeks. He was just quiet and kept to himself. Complete opposite of Zack, who was the most extroverted of all of us. Jay stood off to the side watching the scene with a smirk. He glanced my way, catching my eye, and schooled his features.

I wanted to feel bad for not telling him about Izzy and me, but I didn't. He thought I wasn't right for her. Too old. Too much baggage. I got it. I did. But I wasn't ready to hear it again. Maybe once he saw how happy we were, he would be more okay with it. If not, that was his problem, not mine.

I shook my head and focused back on the truck, sighing when the alarms went off a few minutes later.

After two more calls, I collapsed back on the sofa, stretching out. My phone vibrated and I pulled it out, smiling as I clicked on the text notification from Izzy. I held back the groan that wanted to slip out from the selfie that filled my screen. Izzy, blonde curls falling down around her shoulders, a mischievous spark in her eyes, and the only thing covering her breasts was a bright pink, very tiny bikini top.

Jesus. My dick jumped in my pants.

I ignored the desire pumping through my veins and typed out a message.

Me: Where are you?

Great, Logan. Now you sound like an overbearing parent.

Izzy: Lounging by the pool at my parents house. I stopped by to help my mom with a few things.

Me: Wish I was there.

Izzy: Not sure we'd get away with much with my parents here. Lol

> Me: Oh trust me, I can be very sneaky when I need to be.

> Me: And we both know you can be quiet when you need to be.

Izzy: ☺

> Me: Just wait until I have you all to myself tonight.

Izzy: Food first. You promised I could cook for you tonight.

> Me: I remember. And you promised I could have you for dessert.

> Me: Wear a dress. No panties.

Izzy: And what if I don't?

> Me: Only good girls get rewarded, remember?

That tingle on the back of my head, like I was being watched, made me look up. Jay stood in the kitchen, leaning back against the counter, arms crossed over his chest as he narrowed his eyes at me. Did he suspect we were together? If he asked me again, I wouldn't lie to him. At least not directly.

When the alarms went off again, we all groaned. Today was going to be one of those days. We didn't mind the calls, but when there were multiple ones back-to-back, it could be exhausting. Sometimes physically, and other times it could feel mentally draining as well. Today ended up being busy with simple, routine calls that left most of us dragging. But at least the arsonist was still in the wind and not setting fires.

The exhaustion evaporated by the time I left the station that night. Knowing I was headed home and Izzy was there waiting for me only left me with excitement. I did mentally brace myself for Jay to say something when I changed into jeans and a Henley after taking my shower, but that proved to be a fruitless worry. Either he was too exhausted to ask, or he was waiting for a better time for both of us.

I parked my truck in the drive, entered the house from the side door, and froze. Izzy, long blonde curls cascading down her back, swayed her hips to the music playing from her phone as she stood at the stove. The aroma of something Italian wafted through the air. I set my bag down and shut the door, moving further into the kitchen.

She glanced over her shoulder at me with a smile that stole the air from my lungs. I stepped up behind her, placing my hands on her hips and bringing us flush together, matching her rhythm and moving us to the music.

My dick jumped, hardening against her ass. I fought the urge to lift her dress, bend her over the closest surface, and sink into her soft, wet pussy.

Her head fell back against my shoulder, and I skimmed her ear with my lips, eliciting a moan from her.

"Food first," she whispered.

"I know." I smiled, getting the impression she was reminding herself as much as she was me. "I just wanted to dance with you."

"Yeah?" She pressed back against me and rotated her hips, rubbing against my cock.

"Trying to tease me?"

"Maybe." She smiled. The oven beeped and she lifted her head back up. "Need to get the lasagna in the oven."

I looked over her shoulder at the casserole dish sitting on top of the oven before stepping back and letting her put it inside.

She set the timer and then spun toward me. "That has to bake for about thirty-five minutes, and then I'll need to uncover it."

I took a minute to admire her sundress. It held her breasts with only two thin straps and tied in between before flaring out midway down her stomach. Yellow, with red cherries, it even matched her personality.

"So what you're saying is I can have my dessert first?"

She pulled her bottom lip into her mouth as pink dusted her cheeks.

"Because all I've thought about all day is getting my mouth on you. Feeling you grip my hair as you come on my tongue." I took a step toward her and gripped her waist, bringing her hard against my chest. "You want that, sweetheart?"

"Yes, please," she murmured.

I lifted her and placed her on the granite countertop of the island. "Did you do what I said?"

Her eyes flared as she nodded.

Fuck. "Show me." The words came out husky as I thought about her bare pussy ready for me.

She pulled the hem of her dress up slowly, until it was bunched around her waist, and my fingers dug into her thighs at the sight.

"So fucking perfect." I pushed her legs further apart. "Lay back."

She lowered herself to the counter, and I placed a kiss on the inside of one thigh before doing the same to the other one, hoping the slight scruff on my face would leave its mark.

"Logan." I gripped her hips as they lifted slightly off the counter, keeping her anchored.

"Patience." I trailed my tongue up her leg, stopping so close to where I knew she needed me. "I want to take my time." I repeated the same motion on the other side.

She threaded her fingers into my hair. "Please, don't tease me."

I smiled up at her from between her thighs and licked up her slit. She arched her back, and her fingers tightened in my hair as I explored her with my tongue.

"You like that?"

A breathy moan escaped her. "Yes."

AJ RANNEY

"Good." I covered her clit with my mouth, sucking and flicking back and forth until her moans were echoing around us. I pushed two fingers inside of her and curled them, seeking that spot that I knew would send her flying.

Her grip on my hair tightened. "Oh my God. Right there."

I sucked hard on her clit and spasms racked her body as she screamed out in ecstasy. But I wasn't done, continuing my assault and letting her ride out every wave of her orgasm until she went limp. I placed gentle kisses along her belly and over her hip before helping her sit up and bringing her into my chest.

Holding her, breathing her in, was everything. I could spend forever like this. Dancing in the kitchen and then pleasing her. Even watching her move around my kitchen as she finished making salads to go with the lasagna—it was like she belonged here, had always been here.

I swallowed, my chest suddenly feeling tight.

She looked up, a dusting of pink breaking out across her cheeks. "Why do you keep looking at me like that?"

"Because you're beautiful and I like watching you cook."

I stood up and headed to the wine rack that sat on top of my fridge. "White or red?"

"Red...maybe the Pinot Noir?"

I poured us each a glass and helped her carry the plates to the table. As we sat and ate, we talked about the girls' first soccer game coming up on Saturday and how Jesse, Maggie's boyfriend, planned to be there too. I also thought about the surprise I had for Izzy after the game.

"How was your shift today?"

I blinked, the sudden change of conversation bringing me out of my thoughts. "It was busy. But only a bunch of small crap." I went on to tell her about some of the calls. Having someone to talk to at the end of the day wasn't something I thought I was missing, but sitting here with her chatting about my day felt perfect.

"I think Seth is settling in better now." I smirked. "Although he still doesn't really smile."

She chuckled. "I could've said the same about you."

I paused with my fork halfway to my mouth. "I smile."

"Now you do. But before all you did was glare and growl at me."

I huffed out a laugh. "Oh. Yeah, well, that was extenuating circumstances."

She rolled her eyes and I pushed my plate back before asking her about her day. I sat back in my chair and listened to her talk about her day at the hospital and then with the girls.

As she talked, I couldn't stop staring at her, and the realization that I was falling in love with her hit me square in the chest. I just prayed she felt the same.

Chapter Thirty-Three

IZZY

"Yes." I clapped as Nikki stole the ball and headed toward the goal. She stopped a few feet away from it and pulled her foot back before giving the ball a hard kick. I jumped and yelled as it bounced off the net, landing inside the goal.

Maggie and Jesse chuckled.

A blush crept up my neck. I'd met Maggie's boyfriend once or twice over the last few weeks, but it was only in passing when he would show up as I was leaving. "Sorry, I can be a bit competitive."

"A bit?" Logan asked from the other side of me.

"You shush." I sent him a playful glare.

He wrapped his arm around my back and pulled me closer with a hand on my hip. It had been almost a week since that first night together, and I still got butterflies in my stomach every time he touched me. Was it silly I hoped those never went away?

"I'm glad the girls have you to cheer them on," Maggie said with a smile. "They said you two were going on a—"

Logan cleared his throat loudly, cutting her off and narrowing his eyes slightly. "It's a surprise."

I looked up at Logan. He planned on surprising me?

"Oh." Maggie smirked. "Sorry, girls left that part off."

Logan met my gaze. "And no, I'm not telling you."

I stuck out my bottom lip. "No fair."

He pressed his lips to my temple. "Have I ever told you how cute you are when you pout?"

With a roll of my eyes, I focused back on the game. Although I didn't miss the smile Maggie gave us as she watched our exchange.

Once the game was over, Maggie and Jesse left with the girls, and we had settled back in Logan's truck, curiosity got the best of me.

"Okay. So where are we going?"

"You'll find out when we get there."

I huffed and his lips twitched. I actually didn't mind surprises, but I had to admit I was overly curious about this one.

He reached across and took my hand in his. "How's your mom doing?"

"Stubborn, and doesn't like that she needs help doing certain things right now."

"That's how my mom was when she needed to get a knee replacement last year." He shook his head. "My stepfather had the patience of a saint the whole time. Not sure how he managed."

"Not sure how my dad is doing it either." After a minute of silence, I looked over at him. "What about your dad? You don't talk about him. Is he…"

Logan's jaw locked. Damn it. Obviously, there had to be a reason he didn't talk about him.

"It's okay if you don't want to talk about it."

He shook his head. "He's alive. Lives in California. I don't have much of a relationship with him. He calls and says hi to the girls every now and then."

"Oh." There was so much he wasn't saying.

"It's complicated." A sigh left his lips. "He cheated on my mom." He hesitated before going on. "With someone who watched me as a kid from time to time."

I stared at him with wide eyes. Was that the reason why he never took Jay's suggestion to hire me? Knowing he was attracted to me?

He stole a quick glance my way before returning his focus to the road. "He left us to start a new family. I was pretty much an adult when he finally decided he wanted to try to fix things between us. I wasn't interested. But I went through the motions for my mom because she wanted me to forgive him like she did."

"But you haven't?"

He shrugged. "My mom is better off now with someone who truly cares about her, so in a way I have, but not enough that I want a close relationship with him."

I nodded. "Yeah, that makes sense."

"It does?" He glanced over at me, brows slightly raised. "Most people think I should try harder."

"I think everyone is different and needs to make decisions based on what they want, what they can handle, what makes them happy."

His body visibly relaxed, and his grip loosened on the wheel. "He had a trust set up in my name, but I refuse to touch it. My mom says I'm being petty. It was also a point of contention when Maggie and I were married. We ended up compromising and transferring it over to the girls so they'll get it one day."

"I think that's reasonable." I nodded. "I'm assuming you can access it if you need to?"

"Yeah. I'm the trustee, so I can access it anytime as long as it's used for them."

He turned into a small parking lot, and I gasped when I saw

the sign for scenic helicopter tours. "You're taking me on a helicopter?"

"Is that ok?"

I stared at him with my mouth hanging open. A few nights ago, a show we were watching together depicted tourists going on one, and I mentioned always wanting to ride on a helicopter. I couldn't believe he remembered, or that he listened that intently.

"You serious? Like for real?"

He smiled. "Yes. You said you always wanted to do this."

Never in my wildest dreams did I think I would. Or that someone would do this for me.

"Isn't it expensive?"

He shrugged like it wasn't a big deal. "It's worth it. They'll take us over the mountains and lake. Views are gorgeous."

He parked the truck and climbed out. I waited for him to come around to my side, and when he opened my door, I took his hand and slid out. We both knew I could jump out on my own, but I thought it was sweet he wanted to help me. His fingers threaded through mine, and we headed toward the small building.

By the time we were seated next to each other in the back of the helicopter, headsets on, adrenaline pumped through my veins. Logan leaned closer, and his warm breath whispered along my ear. "Excited or nervous?"

"Excited." I giggled. "Maybe a little nervous."

He wrapped one arm around my shoulders and pulled me closer into his side. Seeing the view of the mountains that surrounded Half Moon Lake amazed me, an experience I was sure I'd never forget. The pilot pointed out the spot where a famous movie was filmed and other well-known landmarks, as well as some I wasn't familiar with.

"Oh my God, look." I pointed out the small window as we flew over the town I grew up in. "That's my high school." After a minute, I spotted the river that separated Half Moon Lake and my town. "And there's the river."

Logan smiled at me. "We're about to fly over the lake."

A heartbeat later, the large crescent-shaped lake came into view.

"There's The Dock," I said, pointing out the window again. "Oh, and look, the beach with the big water slide. We should take the girls sometime this summer. That slide is so much fun."

"They'd love that." He pressed his lips to my temple. "I'm enjoying watching you experience this."

I turned toward him. "Thank you for doing this. It's literally the most exciting thing I've ever done."

Before I knew it, we were landing, and the tour was over. I bounced with excitement as we walked to the truck, skipping ahead before spinning back toward him.

"That was amazing." I took two steps, closing the distance, and wrapped my arms around his neck. "Thank you for bringing me here."

He bent his knees and locked his arms around my back, lifting me off the ground to bring me eye level with him. His mouth slanted over mine, leaving me breathless, and my core hummed with desire.

I pulled back. "Take me home, Logan."

His lips lifted slightly. "Didn't you want to grab dinner?"

I shook my head. "I need you." I'd never felt such intense desire like this with anyone I'd dated. But being with him was quickly becoming an addiction. "Now. Dinner after."

His pupils blew wide, making his caramel-colored eyes almost black. He loosened his arms and let me slide slowly down his body, his hard cock pressing along my belly.

"I will always give you what you need, sweetheart." His gaze burned into me. "Let's go home."

Home. The idea that one day his home would be our home settled over me like a warm blanket, images of what that would look like flashing through my mind. Lounging in bed together on a lazy Saturday morning, making breakfast together as a family, piling in the car to go to a soccer game, going to The Dock for lunch. All of it overwhelmed me, leaving me feeling like I was floating.

I pulled out of his arms and sent him a saucy smile. He raised an eyebrow.

"I'll race you."

His lips twitched. "And what do I get if I win?"

My stomach flipped at the ideas that raced through my mind. "Anything you want."

"Anything?"

I nodded, pulling my bottom lip between my teeth.

He angled his head in the direction of the truck. "I'll give you a head start."

Giggling, I turned and took off at a sprint. I was almost to the truck when large, muscular arms wrapped around my waist, lifting me off the ground.

"Got you," he whispered against my ear. "Now, for my reward."

"And what's that?"

"You'll see." He set me down and opened the passenger door.

Excitement and desire mixed as I climbed into my seat. Once he pulled out onto the main road, he reached over and trailed his fingers up my thigh. I gasped when they disappeared beneath the hem of my knit shorts and swung my gaze over to him. The mischievous smile he wore said he knew exactly what he was doing.

My hips bucked as he rubbed my clit through my lacy thong. "Logan," I moaned.

His touch softened to a torturous degree, and I rotated my hips, trying to find more friction.

His movements froze. "Nope. You have to stay completely still." He cocked a brow at me. "Anything I want, remember? And I want you begging for my cock by the time we get home."

I bit down on my bottom lip, not about to admit I wanted to beg for it now. His ministrations started again, and I let my head fall back against the headrest and closed my eyes. I focused on staying still as his fingers slid under my panties, brushing lightly across my clit. The pressure was just strong enough to send little zaps of pleasure radiating through my body, but not enough to cause an orgasm.

"So wet." He slid two fingers down, toying with my entrance. "You're going to be so ready, begging for me to fuck you, aren't you?"

I twisted my head to the side to look at him and gave him a slight nod.

He continued playing with me, backing off the amount of pressure I needed, but I couldn't deny it felt amazing. I gripped the handle of the door tightly as he increased the speed of his fingers, alternating soft and firm touches. My chest heaved, and another moan left my lips. Without my permission, my hips bucked off the seat. Jesus. Maybe I was going to come.

He paused again. "So needy."

I bit into my lip and pinched my eyes closed, thanking my lucky stars when he moved his fingers again. After a few more minutes of pure torture, he removed his hand.

"What..." My eyelids flew open, and I looked over at him as he turned the truck into his driveway.

Pushing the button on the roof of his truck to open the garage, he pulled in and immediately hit the button again to close the door. The engine off, his hands went to the buckle of his belt.

"Take those off." He motioned at my shorts. "Then get your ass over here."

He reached down and lifted the lever, throwing his seat further back. Hastily, I discarded my shorts and thong and climbed over the center console. I straddled his legs, looking down as his long, thick cock jutted out.

"My turn." I grasped him in my hand and moved up and down, using my thumb to spread his precum over the tip.

He threw his head back with a groan. "Fuck, sweetheart. Keep that up and I'm going to come in your hand instead of inside of you."

I smiled and did it again. "You teased me, so it's only fair I get to tease you now."

His jaw locked, and his eyes became hooded out as I moved my hand slowly up and down. I enjoyed watching him hold onto his control. When his hips bucked, I let go of him. In one quick movement, I lifted up, moving over him, and slid down his length. A moan left my lips as he stretched me until I was fully seated.

"You're not allowed to move this time." I pressed my palms against his chest and rotated my hips, seeking that sweet spot.

"Christ." His fingers dug into my ass, but otherwise, he relaxed back against the seat, letting me take control. "I want to watch your tits bounce."

I slid one strap of my tank top down my arm, repeating the same on the other side. He tugged the fabric down until my breasts were fully exposed, and goose bumps broke out along my skin as his thumbs flicked my nipples.

Between playing with me on the drive home and now feeling him inside me as he played with my nipples, it was all too much. But also not enough. I didn't want to rush this. Being with him, feeling him inside me, was intense, and I swung between wanting to take it slow and wanting to ride him hard and fast.

I started slowly, rising up and sliding back down, rotating my hips so my clit grinded against his pelvis. He kept his gaze locked on my face, and I couldn't look away. Every clench of his jaw and groan that slipped between his lips spurred me on as I increased my speed.

"*Fuuck*," he growled. "Just like that." He reached up and tangled his hand in my hair, tugging slightly.

The sensation shot straight to my core, increasing the pleasure, and my movements became more erratic, grinding against him over and over.

He pulled my mouth down to his and thrust his tongue inside, exploring every crevice. The new angle put more pressure on my clit and I rubbed shamelessly against him. He dug his fingers into my ass, encouraging me to move faster.

I felt so out of control, bombarded with so many sensations as his mouth continued to assault mine, his hand still in my hair, and his fingers digging into my ass. Not to mention the feeling of him stretching me. It all sent me flying. I pulled back, digging my nails into his chest, and my body trembled as my orgasm overtook me.

A growl vibrated through his chest and tumbled from his lips as he exploded, filling me with his release. I slowed my movements but didn't stop, riding out every wave, not ready for it to be over.

Fully spent and sated, I sagged back down onto his chest and lay my head on his shoulder. His arms wrapped around my back, and we stayed like that until our breathing evened out.

His cock twitched and hardened inside of me again, and I sat up, giggling, and stared down at him.

His lips lifted into a seductive smirk. "I can never get enough of you."

"Yeah?" I tilted forward and brushed my lips over his.

I had to admit I'd become just as addicted to the passion that blazed between us. How we couldn't even wait to get inside to do it again. But it was so much more than sex. The way I felt connected with him, the way his touch felt like it was branding my soul. That was what I craved.

Chapter Thirty-Four

LOGAN

I CHECKED MY PHONE AGAIN, waiting for Izzy to text me back. I fucking missed her. We were like two ships passing in the night for the last two days. We spent Tuesday morning together while the girls were at school, but that night started a three-night rotation of night shifts. With her working at the hospital today, I only got to see her for a little bit before I got called in for my shift. Luckily, I only had one more night shift after tonight.

I closed my eyes, attempting to get some sleep, but popped them back open when my phone alerted me to a notification. It was the smoke detector app again.

Damnit. Why would she be baking this late? I clicked on the notification.

What the fuck? The app said it was the apartment above the garage.

The lights came on in the bunk room a second before the alarms blared loudly through the station, and my stomach bottomed out. I jumped up and moved through the space, feeling like a ton of bricks settled in my stomach.

"It's my house," I announced to the guys, not even stopping to answer their questions. "Izzy and the girls are there. We need to go."

I didn't need the dispatcher to tell me it was my house. I knew. Hearing it through the radio only intensified the fear coursing through my veins. I did this every day—hustle down to the bay and slide into my boots and pants—but today it felt like I couldn't move fast enough.

"Murray." Owen held open the door to one of the smaller utility vehicles as he studied me. "You good to drive?"

Was he shitting me? I locked my jaw and nodded.

"Just making sure."

I climbed up in the driver's seat, and Jay turned to me once he was seated in the passenger seat.

"Izzy is smart and my dad drilled fire safety into us and what to do in an emergency. She'll get them out, don't worry."

I nodded. I didn't doubt she'd do what needed to be done to keep everyone safe. The garage was detached, so depending on how bad the fire was, it might not even spread to the house. But the thing I kept getting hung up on was how a fire in the garage apartment could even start. Had to be something electrical. Only thing that kind of made sense was a mouse or something chewing through a wire, leaving it exposed.

All the air left my lungs as I turned the rig down my street and spotted Izzy and the girls standing out by the road, huddled together. As I got closer, I saw Hattie Williams standing with them, too. Honestly, it looked like half the neighborhood was on the street. The main house wasn't showing signs of fire from what I could see, and I breathed a little easier at that.

I pulled the rig up in front of the house and jumped out just as Dylan's SUV pulled up too. Izzy and my daughters sprinted toward me, and I wrapped them in a tight hug.

After a few seconds, I gripped Izzy by the shoulders and pulled her back to look down at her. "Gotta help get the fire out."

She nodded and stepped back, taking the girls with her. I wanted to continue to hold her. Tell her it was all okay. That they were safe and that was all that mattered. But I also had a job to do.

I went through the motions. The steps we always took when putting out a fire. But I was only half there. The other half of me couldn't stop thinking about how much worse it could have been. What it could have cost me if the fire had spread. This was why I had the smart system for fire protection. Neither Izzy nor myself might have known about the fire until it was too late. That thought sat heavy in my gut.

It didn't take long to put it out given it was mainly the open space of the living room and kitchen, and once we were sure it was out, I sent Izzy and the girls back inside while we started the over-haul process. I thought Alice and Nikki would be more freaked out, but Izzy exuded calmness and ushered them back inside without an issue. I loved that they trusted her and found comfort with her.

I stood in the middle of the small space with Jay and Owen, looking around for what might have caused the fire. I tried not to assess the value of the damage as the weird burn pattern that indicated multiple points of origin caught my attention.

"Fuck," Owen muttered seeing the same thing I did.

I didn't want to believe it when it looked like the door had been jimmied open. But looking at the burn patterns, there was no denying this was arson.

"He's sending you a message." Jay glanced over at me. "He must know you're the one who found the matchbook at that BBQ joint."

I swallowed, seeing the fear in his eyes that probably matched my own. Was this just a warning? Would the next time put Izzy and the girls in more danger? I couldn't let that happen. But I couldn't be with them all the time either, so what else could I do?

I tried not to think about all that as I stepped back inside the house, telling the guys I needed a few minutes to make sure everyone was good.

"Hey," I said as Izzy came down the stairs. I wrapped my arms around her as she barrelled into my chest. "Girls in bed?"

She nodded against my chest and I held her for a heartbeat before she pulled back. "Want to go up and see them before they fall asleep again?"

"Yeah." I nodded and pressed my lips to her forehead. "I'll only be a minute." I took the stairs two at a time and headed into their room.

They were both tired with fluttering, sleepy eyes. As I gave them each a kiss and promised to see them first thing in the morning, they asked if I would send Izzy up to stay with them. Easy request to grant, and once again, I was grateful they had her and felt safe with her. Because I wouldn't be able to leave them otherwise.

Once back downstairs, I pulled Izzy into my embrace, but groaned when the tones of an incoming call came through the radio.

"Sorry..." I started.

She shook her head as she stepped back. "I understand. Duty calls."

Her smile was genuine, and although I didn't want to go, we both knew I had to.

Chapter Thirty-Five

IZZY

I WAITED IMPATIENTLY for Logan to walk in the door. I really needed to get lost in his embrace, his touch. After the stress of last night, I needed to feel his strong arms around me, his lips on mine. I understood why he couldn't hang around last night, and the last thing I wanted to be was needy. But with how tightly wound his body seemed, it was obvious he needed comfort, too.

He'd told me to let the girls sleep as long as I could since I'd had to wake them up to get them outside. So I waited with one ear listening for the kids, and the other for Logan. Finally, the sound of his truck rumbled down the driveway, and I ran to the side door and swung it open. I went down the two steps, stopping on the sidewalk, and waited for him to get out.

He paused a few feet away. His body language reminded me

of those first few days when I started working for him. Rigid, jaw locked, completely closed off.

"The girls still sleeping?" he asked.

I nodded. "Yeah."

"We need to talk."

I swallowed. Somehow, I didn't think I was going to like this conversation.

"Everything okay?"

"No." He shook his head. "I want you to take the girls to Maggie's."

I tilted my head. "Yeah... that's already the plan. After school starts her two days with them."

He clenched his jaw. "I mean, they're going to stay with Maggie until it's safe enough to be here."

What did he mean safe enough?

I opened my mouth to ask, but he went on. "That fire last night was the arsonist. The one setting fires all over town. He knows I'm the one who pointed the investigators to him, and I can't have you guys here—"

"Wait..." I blinked, trying to process everything he was telling me. "You're sending me away, too?"

He shifted. "I don't have any other choice. He's targeting me now, and next time it might be the actual house. I refuse to put you and the girls in danger."

I wanted to argue. Yell at him. Stomp my feet. But I knew that wouldn't change anything. With his back ramrod straight and the way his jaw kept clenching, he was bracing for resistance. I wanted him to trust in me, in us, but I also needed him to do that on his own. And to do that, he needed to know I could handle the life he had. If I forced his hand, he would just stress and worry.

I sighed. "Okay."

His eyes widened slightly. "It's only until they catch this guy."

With a clipped nod, I crossed my arms. "Okay." The sound of my name came from inside the house. "Better get them fed and off to school."

I spun, trying to ignore the sadness that overcame me. His fear drove his reactions. I got that. And for now, I could go along with this plan to ease his worry. But this wasn't a long-term solution, and eventually he needed to see that.

But still, my mind whirled with questions. What if we were living together? Or married? Would he still choose to send me away without even asking me what I wanted or what I thought? Would he single-handedly make decisions about our life, about what was best for us? For the girls? I understood we weren't there yet, but until this was resolved, I knew those thoughts would continue to plague me.

Chapter Thirty-Six

LOGAN

I T   H A D   B E E N   A L M O S T five days since that Thursday morning when I sent Izzy and my girls away. It was what I'd decided, so I had no right to be miserable. But fuck did I miss them.

I'd video-called with Nikki and Alice once or twice and came to their soccer game on Saturday. Honestly, it wasn't much different than when they were with Maggie for long stretches, but the idea of this going on for weeks or months made my gut twist.

I'd texted and called Izzy every day, and we grabbed lunch after the soccer game. She didn't seem angry, but I could tell she was holding back. I'd expected her to yell at me when I told her my plan. But she didn't. Not sure if that made it worse or better. I couldn't tell if she was mad at me or not, and there wasn't much I could do to fix it if she was. Keeping her and the girls safe was my priority. I had to hope she understood that.

I wiped the front of the rig with the rag. This was the third time I'd wash the damn thing since the fire above my garage. Something about the task calmed my racing thoughts. Usually. Today, it wasn't really helping.

Jay appeared in my peripheral vision, standing silently, watching me.

I turned to him with a raised brow. Was this the conversation where he would tell me his sister deserved better? Because right now, I might agree with him. She didn't deserve to be dealing with a serial arsonist who had decided I was the problem.

"Spit it out." I threw the rag down in the soapy bucket. "Let me guess. You're pissed I'm dating your sister because she deserves better than the life I can give her."

He flinched back. "Dude. I was just coming to see how you're holding up. This situation sucks and you're both miserable."

I narrowed my eyes at him before finally relenting and sitting down on the bumper of the rig. "She's really miserable?"

"Definitely wasn't like herself last night when she stopped by to visit."

God, I hated this. For both of us. "Not sure what else I can do. You even said yourself the arsonist is sending me a message. I refuse to put her and the girls in harm's way."

"What does Izzy think?"

"What do you mean?"

"Have you guys talked about what you're going to do if this keeps going?"

I stared blankly at him. "No."

Truthfully, I had no idea what the answer was. I missed Izzy and my girls, and it'd only been five days. I didn't even want to imagine how I'd feel if this went on for more than another week or so.

He let out a huff and shook his head at me. "That explains why she wasn't forthcoming last night about the whole thing."

"You think she's mad?"

He shrugged. "Women expect us to use our words. I've even learned that, and you're older than me. And you were married."

I ran a hand down my face. "I need to know they're safe. That he can't get to them."

"Yeah, man. I get that. But you have no idea if this is going to go on for weeks or even months. Are you going to keep them away that long?"

"What else can I do? I can't be there with them all the time. What if he tries setting my actual house on fire next time?"

Jay stared at me for a long minute before speaking again. "Everything we've seen so far says this kid isn't trying to hurt anyone."

I glared at Jay, knowing what he meant but not liking it. "He's twenty, not a kid. And setting anything on fire runs the risk of getting someone hurt."

Jay's gaze softened. "I know, I just meant he's not intentionally trying to hurt people. He could have set your house on fire, but he knew people were inside."

"I don't want him anywhere near my house, Izzy, or the girls."

"Then get one of those crazy-ass security systems Dylan has. You'd be alerted if anyone gets close enough."

"Already ahead of you. Someone comes out tomorrow to install it."

He smiled. "That's good. Now you need to talk to Izzy and actually discuss what you should do next. Communicate and make a plan together as a team."

I sighed and let my head fall forward, cradling it in my hands. Now that I thought about it, sending them away should have been more of a conversation, not me making a unilateral decision for everyone. I expected her to push back, and was so relieved when she agreed so easily, I just went with it.

"And for the record, I think my sister deserves someone who

will protect her, take care of her, and make her happy. From what she's said over the last two weeks, that's you. And I have no problem with it." He smirked. "As long as you don't break her heart, because then I'll have to kick your ass."

"Wait…" I tilted my head. "You've known we were together the whole time?"

It was clear the night of the fire we were together, and I figured he suspected something in the weeks before, but I had no clue Izzy had confirmed it.

"My sister is an oversharer and doesn't keep a secret well, so, yes. I got an earful the night we drove together to the hospital, and at least three conversations about how things were going since then."

An exasperated huff left my mouth as I stared at him. "Why didn't you say something?"

"It was more fun watching you sweat." He shrugged. "She loves you and made it clear I needed to get on board. So this is me getting on board."

"She told you that?" My chest warmed at the idea she loved me. Because, fuck, I loved her so much it hurt.

His lips twitched. "She didn't need to. I've never seen her this happy with any other guy she's dated."

I glanced at my watch. I still had almost seven hours left on shift. Seven hours before I could see her. Talk to her.

"Take one of the utility vehicles," Jay suggested, easily reading my thoughts. "Adam's here, he can drive the rig if we get a call."

I popped to my feet. "You sure?"

He nodded. "Yeah. I'll go let Owen know. He'll understand."

"Thanks, man." I slapped his shoulder as I moved past him and headed toward the small truck.

I needed to see my girl and tell her how crazy I was about her. And pray she wasn't too mad at me.

Chapter Thirty-Seven

IZZY

I SIGHED as I finished wiping down the counters in my kitchen. The twins were at school and I didn't work at the hospital today, so I had way too much time on my hands. I'd already baked three dozen cookies hoping it would make me feel better, but all it did was remind me of the day I handed a shirtless, sexy-smirking Logan cookies.

I jumped from being irritated with him to being frustrated with myself, and then back to missing him. He wanted to protect me, and I shouldn't be irritated about that. I really did understand why he was keeping us away. But something my brother said last night stuck with me.

"He's protecting his kids and the woman he loves. I'd go to the ends of the earth to protect Nora and Sarah."

It made me smile to think Logan actually loved me, but he hadn't said that yet. He didn't even ask what I thought or what I wanted. That was what actually bothered me. That none of this had been a conversation. I got it in the heat of the moment, and the direct aftermath, but I thought by now we would've talked about what we were going to do moving forward.

A knock came from my front door, and I put the sponge down before heading to answer it. Not sure who would be knocking on my door on a Tuesday in the middle of the day, I almost stumbled back when I opened it to find Logan standing there, hands braced on either side of the doorframe, head slightly bowed.

"Logan?" Did something happen? Maybe they finally caught the guy...or maybe he decided this thing between us wasn't going to work. My stomach twisted painfully at that thought.

He looked up, and in his gaze was so much turmoil. "Can I come in?"

I swallowed, stepping back and waving him in. "Of course." After shutting the door, I crossed my arms over my chest and faced him.

"I messed up." He grabbed the back of his neck. "I wanted to protect you and the girls, but I didn't handle it right. I should have started by telling you I love you, and the thought of anything happening to you or my kids scared the hell out of me."

"I know." My body relaxed, and for the first time in five days, I smiled, hope blooming in my chest. I stepped forward and reached for his hand. "I'm not mad, and I love you too. I understand why you needed to do what you did."

He shook his head and brought my hand up in front of his chest, covering it with both of his. "Sweetheart, if we're going to make this work, we need to be honest with each other. Talk about things. Make decisions together. You may not be angry, but I don't believe that the way I handled things didn't hurt you."

I lowered my head. I wouldn't lie to him. "I did understand, but yes, I was a little hurt. I just wished we would have talked about it. That you would have asked what I wanted."

He reached up and cupped the side of my face with his palm, tilting my head up to look at him. "I promise, from here on out, you and I are a team. There may be times I feel strongly about something, but I will remember to talk it out with you. Include you in the plan and not be an insensitive ass."

I needed to take responsibility for my part, too. "I should have spoken up. But I wanted you to see that I can handle your life. The girls, the hours, even the possible danger. I know you think because I'm young I might see a life with you as being tied down or too much, but being with you and the girls makes me the happiest I've ever been."

He pulled me toward him and wrapped his arms around my shoulders, bringing me flush against his chest. "Jesus. One of the things I love about you is that you speak your mind. Please don't ever allow me to squash that."

I giggled, tightening my arms around his waist. "Good to know." I melted into his hold, not realizing until that moment how much I needed this.

"I missed you so much." He pressed his lips to the top of my head.

"Me too." I pulled back and tilted my head back to look up at him.

He leaned down and captured my mouth, brushing his lips tenderly against mine before pulling back with a smirk. "So there's something else I want to talk to you about."

"Yeah?"

"I want you to move in with me."

My mouth fell open. Was he serious? "You don't think it's too soon?"

His lips twitched. "I'm sure it's what I want. If you need more time, take as long as you need."

"It's what I want too." Although my lease wasn't up until the end of the year because I took it over from Angie halfway through hers. "I might need some time to find someone to take over my lease, though." And I knew exactly the person to ask.

"That's fine. But starting tonight, I don't want to go another night without you in my arms."

Was he not worried about the danger anymore? "What about the arsonist?"

"I'm having a security system installed tomorrow. One like Dylan's, with cameras and motion-activated lights." He studied me for a moment. "We can talk about it more, but I'm not sure I want you guys to be there overnight without me. At least for right now."

I nodded. The security system was a good call. His fingers tangled in my hair, and he claimed my mouth again. God, I missed his kisses, the way he always left me a desperate puddle of goo.

I trailed my fingers up his back. "How long do you have before you have to get back?"

A sexy smirk lifted his lips. "Missed my cock?"

I nodded. "Very much so." But more than just the pleasure he gave me, I missed feeling connected with him like I did when we were together.

Our gazes locked, and something powerful passed between us. Like he knew exactly what I wanted.

He bent his knees and grabbed me by my ass, lifting me into his arms. I wrapped my legs around his waist and giggled as he turned and headed down the hallway.

"We'll have to make it quick." He threw me on my bed, and his hands went to the buckle of his pants.

I quickly stripped out of my one-piece romper and gasped when he grabbed my ankles, pulling me to the edge of the bed.

"You ready for me?"

I nodded and he ran the tip of his cock through my wetness, spreading it before inching so slowly into me I thought I might die.

"Fuck, sweetheart." He stared down at me with so many emotions swirling in his irises. "So perfect."

Once he was fully seated, we both let out a moan. He stilled, gaze locked on my face. I couldn't look away. The intensity in his eyes, the unguarded vulnerability. The love I could plainly see. All of it left me breathless.

His hands trailed up my thighs, over my hips, and gripped my waist. He slowly drew back and slammed back in. With each thrust, my body lit up with not only sensations of pleasure but the love I felt for him, too. Tears burned behind my eyes and I closed them, focusing on where we were joined and the pleasure he was giving me.

"Sweetheart, look at me."

I swallowed and opened my eyes.

He brushed the hair back from my forehead. "I got you."

The words were simple, but the meaning behind them was so much more. And even though we both knew we didn't have a lot of time, his thrusts were slow and unhurried like we had all the time in the world. Neither of us wanted to rush. Instead, we wanted to savor every moment.

He grabbed my hands and pinned them to the mattress on either side of my head, leaning down so he was only a few inches from my face. His stare was so intent, as if he was storing every detail to memory.

We didn't speak, yet so much was being said. We were barely moving, staring at each other as he slowly rocked into me. I felt treasured in that moment with him. Being with him always felt different, and now I understood why. It wasn't sex. Even from that first time, it was always making love.

The emotions overwhelmed me, intensifying everything, and I embraced them. I let myself feel it all. It only added to being with him. The first waves of pleasure started low in my gut and threatened to overtake me as I fought to hang on. Fought to draw out this moment with him.

"Logan," I moaned.

"Got you," he repeated.

And those two words sent me soaring. He leaned down and took my mouth in an all-consuming kiss as I came harder than I ever had, and he followed me over the edge a second later.

His movements slowed as we both came down from the high. He pulled out and collapsed down next to me, bringing me into his side and pressing a kiss to the top of my head.

"Jesus. That was fucking amazing."

I smiled. "Intense."

He rolled us so he hovered above me and cupped my cheek with his hand, searching my face. "I love you," he whispered.

I reached up and ran my fingers through his hair. "I love you, too."

He leaned down and claimed my mouth, his warm lips running back and forth over mine until the tones of the radio interrupted the moment. He rested his forehead against mine and sighed heavily.

"I hate that I have to leave you."

"I'll see you tonight." I gave him one last kiss before he rolled off me and stood up, fixing his pants.

He stared down at my naked body and groaned. "I'll pick you up for dinner after I get off work."

I raised a brow, and he chuckled.

"If that's okay with you? Or you can meet me at the house if you want to do dinner at home."

Home. Warmth blossomed in my chest at the idea that would be our home.

"Dinner out is fine. As long as we're together, it doesn't matter to me."

He smiled and placed another quick kiss on my lips before he was gone. I lay there for far too long, basking in the happiness that embraced me.

Being with him was so much more than I ever thought was possible.

Chapter Thirty-Eight

LOGAN

WALKING in my front door and smelling the aroma of something delicious had been something I'd gotten used to over the last few weeks. But the sight that greeted me was definitely not. The lights were on in the foyer, but the rest of the house sat in darkness. Izzy and the girls were here. My security cameras tracked them coming home after school and not leaving again, so I knew they were here.

Having the cameras and security system installed had definitely eased my worries. But investigators still haven't been able to get enough evidence to arrest the fucker. He was still out there, but hadn't set another fire since my garage last month.

I set my bag down and walked further through the house. As I entered the kitchen, the lights flicked on and Izzy and the girls jumped out, letting go of balloons and yelling, "Surprise!"

I told her not to do anything special for my birthday. Somehow, I wasn't surprised she didn't listen. I couldn't help but smile as I took in the banner that hung over the archway to the great room, all the bunches of balloons that were tied to various other places, and still more that floated along the ceiling.

"Happy birthday, Daddy." Nikki ran toward me and wrapped her arms around my legs.

I picked her up in one arm before Alice made her way toward me and I repeated the motion, bringing them both up in my arms. "Thank you."

"We made you a cake." Alice beamed proudly.

I found Izzy's gaze and she smirked. I swear she and her baked goods were going to be the death of me.

She shrugged. "Can't have a birthday without cake."

I could only pray dinner wasn't loaded down with carbs as well.

"Thank you." I looked at Nikki and then over to Alice. "I bet it's delicious."

"Can we have cake first?"

"I already told you two no." Izzy jumped in. "We need to eat dinner first."

The girls' lips both turned down into pouts. "But..."

"Izzy's right. Dinner first, no buts."

"Fine." They both sighed, and I fought a smirk as I set them back down.

They ran over to the table and took their seats as I closed the distance between Izzy and me, gripping her by the waist and pulling her against my body. She popped up on her toes and pressed a quick kiss against my lips. The girls giggled from the table and I smiled.

"Happy birthday, papa bear," Izzy whispered.

I leaned down, my lips close to her ear. "Where's my present?"

When she'd asked me last week what I wanted, I sent her sexy lingerie decked out with stockings and garters.

"Hmm." Her breath skated across the skin of my neck. "I might be wearing it."

My dick jumped, pressing against her belly. Her giggle did nothing to mitigate the situation. I closed my eyes and tried imagining five things that I found the opposite of her in sexy lingerie.

"Can we eat now?" Nikki asked from the table.

I swallowed down the groan that wanted to slip through my lips, took another deep breath, and turned us toward the table.

"Meatloaf?" I eyed the table set with plates and food.

"Yep." Izzy took her chair. "Don't worry, I made it without breadcrumbs this time, and there's salad to go with it."

"Thank you. You didn't need to do all this."

She rolled her eyes. "It's just dinner and cake. Not like I threw you a party or anything."

"But I thought—" Alice started before Izzy narrowed her eyes at her. "Oh. Right."

Great. I had a feeling I was getting a birthday party tomorrow. I wrapped my arm around Izzy and leaned over, pressing a kiss to her temple.

"You're amazing and I love you."

She turned her head slightly with a smirk. "Hopefully that's still true after tomorrow."

I stared into her eyes. "It will always be true. Forever."

Epilogue

IZZY

I PARKED my car in front of the firehouse and gathered the bags of food from the back seat before getting out. I enjoyed preparing lunch or dinner for the guys when I was able to. I knew they all appreciated it, and it gave me a chance to spend time with Logan when he was on shift.

As I made my way toward the door of the firehouse, Lyla jumped out of the back of the ambulance that was parked in front of the bay.

She sent me a smile. "Hey, what are you doing here?"

"Bringing lunch for the guys." I shifted the bag in my left arm. "They're still not back yet?"

Logan had texted almost an hour ago saying they were

finishing up, and I dropped the girls off at Maggie's with her new nanny before coming straight here.

"No, they're still at the old Miller farm. Should be back any minute, though. They were wrapping up when we left." She reached her arms out. "Here, I'll help you carry all this up."

I passed off a few of the bags and followed behind her. We put everything away in the fridge, just in case they got another call and didn't make it back here right away.

"You and Mia all moved in?" I still wasn't sure how they were sharing a one-bedroom. But both of them were looking for a place for different reasons. Mia was slightly more reluctant. Surprisingly, not about sharing a bedroom, but about the love curse everyone was convinced existed over the apartment. The guys wished Seth would take it. According to Logan, they thought getting laid would reduce his grumpiness. They were all ridiculous.

"Yeah, we finished moving everything in this weekend." The tones of a call coming in blared loudly. "Duty calls," she said with a smile before turning and heading back downstairs.

I stood frozen, listening to the dispatcher advise there was an active fire at the Miller farm. Logan and Lyla said the fire was out and they were wrapping up. Did it restart? When the dispatcher added that two were trapped inside, I gasped and began moving to the stairs that led down to the main floor. My heart took off at a sprint, beating hard in my chest. As I cleared the last step, the ambulance pulled away from the building.

I couldn't sit here and wait. What if Logan was one of the ones trapped? I needed to know he was okay. I typically didn't stress or worry about this stuff, but most of the time I didn't know about the close calls until after it was over.

It took less than ten minutes to make it to the scene, but those short minutes felt like forever. I raced to where everyone was gathered, looking one way and then the other, trying to spot Logan.

"Izzy?"

I turned, and my body sagged in relief at the sight of him jogging toward me. "Oh, thank God," I mumbled.

"What are you doing here, sweetheart?" he asked once he got closer.

I rushed into his arms and wrapped my arms around his back, holding him tight.

He chuckled. "Did you miss me that much?"

"I heard the call." I pulled back to look up at him. "They said two people were stuck inside?"

His expression turned serious, and he pressed his lips against my forehead. "Not me. Seth and Violet."

Oh no. I swallowed.

And if Violet was here, that meant she was collecting evidence. That meant the arsonist was at it again. Damn it. We were all hopeful that two months of quiet meant he was done. I turned toward the old farmhouse that was now almost completely engulfed in flames.

Logan draped his arm over my shoulder and pulled me into his side. The sound of wood splintering echoed around us a second before part of the house collapsed on one side. I leaned further into Logan's side, comforted by his embrace, and sent a silent prayer up for Seth and Violet.

Ready to find out what happens with Seth and Violet? Make sure to preorder the next book in the series!
Out of the Fire

More By A J Ranney

Half Moon Lake Series:

Always Yours (book 1)

Wishing to be Yours (book 1.5)

Impossibly Yours (book 2)

Imperfectly Yours (book 3)

Bravely Yours (book 3.5)

Recklessly Yours (book 4)

Half Moon Lake Heroes: The Red Line

Bravely Yours (book 0.5)

Playing with Fire

Out of the Fire

The Line of Fire

Calling a Cease Fire

WRITING AS GRACIE YORK

Goldilocks and the Grumpy Bear

Tumbling Head Over Heels

Along Came The Girl

Peter Pumpkined Out

Back Together Again

Ghost Shoes

Follow Me

Come be apart of my Facebook Group.
AJ's Book Nook

Find me on social media:
Instagram.com/a.j.ranney
Facebook.com/ajranney19
tiktok.com/@ajranney3
Goodreads.com/AJ Ranney
http://www.ajranney.com

Note from the Author

Dear Reader,

THANK YOU for reading *Playing with Fire*. I enjoyed writing Izzy and her carefree look on everything. It offset Logan so well and they turned out to be the perfect pair!

Next I'm working on Seth and Violet's story and then the final two guys at the Half Moon Lake Fire Department!

I appreciate each and every one of you. It's only because people like you read our books that authors like me get to publish them.

Check out my website for bonus content and stay up to date with latest releases.

Love,
AJ Ranney
www.ajranney.com

Acknowledgments

Like always, I need to thank my husband first. He has been one of my biggest cheerleaders, is always willing to listen to what I write, and has done bedtime with the kids more times than I probably realize. I appreciate your eagerness to help me when I'm stuck and your willingness to let me read to you.

And then to my kids, who are always curious about what Mommy is writing. And yes, you still need to wait until you're eighteen to read them. But by then I doubt you'd want to!

Jenn, I know you're sick of my stories by the time we get to this part! Regardless, thank you for dealing with my constant *how do I fix this?* questions and talking me down every time I'm ready to burn everything I write. You're always willing to read and edit multiple times, hold my hand when I need it, and tell me to just do it when I need that too. But above everything you've done, your friendship has meant the world to me.

A HUGE thank you to my author friends who have supported me in so many ways, whether through encouragement or reading my stuff: Annie Charme, Kat Long, Jenni Bara, Brittanee Nicole, Daphne Elliot, Kristin Lee, Amanda Zook, Alexandra Hale and many more!

Also to all my beta readers: thank you for always willing to read and give feedback!

Cami, thank you for all the graphics, reading and helping find teaser lines and the phone calls to chat and get organized. I appreciate all your help!

Michelle, a HUGE thank you goes out to you. Every

comment you left that made me stop and think, even when I wanted to push back. Your guidance really helped shape and mold this book. Thank you for always willing to answer questions or help me talk something out!

Holly, as always, thank you for being my sister, even if not by blood—and to my mom and mother-in-law: You have been so supportive throughout every step of this crazy journey!

And finally, thank you to the rest of my friends and family who have helped or supported me. I used to think it took a village to raise little humans, and that still holds true, but it also takes a village to write and publish a book!

About the Author

A.J. Ranney lives in Maryland with her ever-growing zoo, including two kids, two cats, an attention-loving dog, a bunny, a cricket-eating lizard, and her lovable, well-meaning husband. She likes to leave the chaos of her real world behind and lose herself in a steamy romance novel. Her passion for reading romance prompted her writing journey, leading her to create relatable happily ever afters that come from her own dreams and experiences.

She loves coffee, sushi, wine, and her family. Not necessarily in that order. Her inner peace comes from the water, always relating to her zodiac sign, the Pisces. It's no wonder the small town she created in her stories is situated on a lake.